Rides That Way

Rides That Way

by

Susan Ketchen

OOLICHAN BOOKS
FERNIE, BRITISH COLUMBIA, CANADA
2016

Library and Archives Canada Cataloguing in Publication

Ketchen, Susan, author

    Rides that way / Susan Ketchen.

ISBN 978-0-88982-321-1 (softcover)

      I. Title.

PS8621.E893R53 2017   jC813'.6   C2017-903974-1

Cover design by Vanessa Croome.

We gratefully acknowledge the financial support of the Canada Council for the Arts, the British Columbia Arts Council through the BC Ministry of Tourism, Culture, and the Arts, and the Government of Canada through the Canada Book Fund, for our publishing activities.

Published by
Oolichan Books
P.O. Box 2278
Fernie, British Columbia
Canada V0B 1M0

www.oolichan.com

Printed in Canada

Dedicated with admiration and respect to the Turner Syndrome community, especially to the girls and women who have been generous in answering my questions and recounting their personal experiences.

Chapter One

I am galloping.

We splash out of a pond and ahead of us is a long straight stretch of pastureland with a gradual rise. At the crown, scarcely visible, is a massive log jump, the final obstacle on the course.

I lean forward, loosen the reins, and let Brooklyn go. Kansas, my coach, doesn't like us galloping. She says it's dangerous, that unexpected things happen too fast at high speeds, but we don't have many opportunities where the footing is this great, so I let him run. I don't even have to ask. I raise my butt out of the saddle and set him free. His back drops as he flattens underneath me and the three-beat gait of canter dissolves into four.

It used to be that if I was galloping, it meant I was dreaming. I've been dreaming about riding and galloping for as long as I remember. By the time I was seven, if I found myself riding I knew automatically that I must be dreaming and I'd be so sad about not owning a horse that I'd wake myself crying.

I'm not dreaming this time. I am riding the cross-country phase in my first ever three-phase eventing competition. It's not like my dreams. Real riding is much more difficult than dream riding. I'm panting, my horse is panting, my legs are tired and the reins are slick with sweat from both of us. The one thing that's the same is the exhilaration. I am on top of the world. I am having the time of my life. If I wasn't breathing so hard I would scream.

In some of my dreams I have total control. If I don't like something that's happening, I change it without waking up. Today, on Brooklyn, I have a different kind of control. I feel absolutely connected to my horse and the turf and the air around us. I am alive. I am in the zone. For once in my life I know exactly what I'm doing. Kansas is wrong—galloping is bliss. So far we've jumped the whole course without a refusal or run-out. Every fence was perfect, even the ditches that I was afraid he would fall into, he soared over and carried on like a champion. I am pumped. We are unbeatable.

The final obstacle looms into view and I shorten my reins to gather Brooklyn into balance. He's enjoying galloping as much as I am and doesn't want to slow. He sees the jump and pulls towards it. He is breathing really hard. I've never ridden a jump out of a gallop, and it doesn't feel right. I can't pick his take-off spot. Possibly I could slow him by doing a circle, but if we're in the penalty zone in front of the jump and cross our own path it will be counted as a refusal. Though a refusal may be better than death. I pull hard on the left rein, but he ignores me. I feel like I'm on a runaway train.

This is not good. Dreaming about riding cross-country has one big advantage over the real thing: at least in dreams I can't break my neck.

Brooklyn is a full stride out from the jump when he takes off. I only stay with him by grabbing a handful of mane and hanging on. There's a thud as he clips the log with his front feet. This is not good. I put my weight in my heels and lean back.

Brooklyn stumbles on landing. I brace my hands into the base of his neck. I'm too young to die: I'm only fourteen. Please please, Brooklyn, stay on your feet. The reins slip through my fingers and his head disappears from view as he goes to his knees. There's nothing I can do but hang on and pray he doesn't somersault. I hold my breath as he scrambles beneath me, I try to keep my head up and stay centred and not throw him any more off balance... not here, I don't want to die here, at the last fence, on the best day of my life, I promise I'll never let this happen again, I will never gallop, I will do what my coach tells me, I will do what my parents tell me... and then miraculously he pops up onto all four feet and canters on down the hill. The reins are flapping loose, and I pick them up just in time to guide him through the finish gate.

My cousin Taylor is waiting for me in the end zone. She has agreed to be my groom for this event. She doesn't approve of using animals in competition, so she's there more for Brooklyn than for me. She wants to be sure his spirit is respected and he isn't abused.

As if I would abuse Brooklyn. "We did it," I tell Taylor, panting. "We went clean for the whole course, no refusals." I pause to catch my breath. I'm ready to tell her about every approach, every take-off... except the last one of course.

"Hop down, I'll hold him," says Taylor, grabbing a rein.

I hesitate. It's true, I should dismount so Brooklyn can recover faster, but I don't want to. I want this ride to last as long as possible, if not forever. My whole body pulses with the pleasure of being a competitor on even footing with everyone else. As soon as I dismount I will return to my usual status as a human shrimp.

Taylor slips the stirrup off my foot and tugs the top of my boot. "Come on, Sylvia. Brooklyn needs to rest."

I slide slowly from the saddle. My feet hit the ground. I am still me, the new invincible version. I can hang on to this.

I am busting with details of riding the course. I want to relive every obstacle.

"Taylor, my ride was fantastic. The first jump was easy and he cleared it by a mile, and the approach to the second one was slightly downhill so I—"

"He's so wet," says Taylor. "Look, he's all lathered between his hind legs. Poor Brooklyn!"

She doesn't want to hear. I'll have to wait until I see Kansas, she'll want to know everything.

We strip off Brooklyn's tack and replace his bridle with a halter. The leather crown of the bridle is sticky with sweat. His saddle pad is sodden and has doubled its weight. I've never seen Brooklyn this hot before. He must have tried really hard. We are both competitors. I'm hot too. My face is throbbing, and it must be beet red. My pulse hammers in my ears faster than I've ever heard it. I could use a shower, and a glass of ice water, and a chair in the shade, but Taylor is right, Brooklyn's needs come first and I can wait.

When I bend to peel off his protective front leg boots I see the grass stains on his knees. I check to see if Taylor has noticed, but she has her hand on Brooklyn's cheek and her eyes are closed: she's having an animal communicator moment with him.

"He says he's tired but he's really pleased with himself," she says. "He thought the last jump was really exciting. I'm sorry I missed it."

"You missed it? Oh, that's too bad," I say. I'm so relieved I could faint. If she'd seen it, she'd never forgive me. "And he's right, that last fence was great." Which isn't exactly a lie. Brooklyn was great at getting back on his feet. The less Taylor knows, the better.

"I wasn't watching. I wasn't expecting you yet. You were really early. Could you have gone off course and missed a jump?"

"I don't think so," I say. "He wanted to go pretty fast."

"I'll take him for a walk," says Taylor. "He wants to cool down. We'll sponge him off later." She disappears with him between the trucks and trailers, stroking his neck and telling him what a good horse he is.

For the first time all day, I have nothing to do. This morning we were busy with the dressage phase—where we weren't especially successful because Brooklyn was excited and Kansas says I was unfocussed. We did better in phase two, the stadium jumping. Now, with no penalties on the cross-country, we might even be in contention for a ribbon. Or a trophy! I've always wanted to win a trophy for my riding. I'd never tell Taylor this, of course. Even Kansas insists that competitions are not about the ribbons; they're about improving your performance. Still, a trophy would be fantastic. I can imagine it, gleaming on my window ledge at home, or better yet, on the mantle over the fireplace where the neighbours will see it through the window as they walk by.

Kansas looms in front of me and holds her stopwatch in my face. I guess I won't be reviewing the details of my achievement with her anytime soon.

"Have you seen your time?" she says. "You must have galloped. I told you not to."

"We didn't gallop for long. And he wanted to."

"That's not the point. I told you that you didn't have the core strength to bring him back into balance if he flattened out on you."

Oh—so that's what happened. I have a vague memory of her mentioning this and suggesting I do boring plank exercises like my mom brags about after her Pilates class. Forget that, I'll do exercises for old people when I'm old. "Whatever," I say. "Maybe I'll get some bonus points for speed."

"No, Sylvia, what you'll get are penalty points for going below the speed fault time. It's considered dangerous riding. You'll be out of contention for any ribbons now, not that I care. And that last fence... " She shakes her head. "I thought you were a goner. He could have flipped. I almost had a heart attack." She closes her eyes and massages her forehead with her fingers, leaving wavy lines of smudged dirt on her skin. "You... oh, never mind." She turns and stomps away. What was I supposed to say? Is she angry or frightened or what?

Kansas never used to be emotional like this, but she is colossally pregnant and little things bother her a lot. I don't think she's getting enough sleep.

The glow is fading from my perfect day. I don't care about not getting a ribbon, but I don't like it if Kansas is upset with me. And what worries me most is what will happen when Taylor finds out I've been penalized for dangerous riding. In retrospect, I don't think what I did was dangerous, we did survive after all, and mostly it was Brooklyn's idea, but that won't matter.

Taylor won't let this go. Animal welfare is a huge thing for her. She's a maniac about it, in her quiet spiritual way.

I am in deep trouble, and then the situation gets worse.

Rushing towards me, arms spread wide for a hug, is my mom.

"Oh, Honey!"

"I thought you weren't coming," I mumble as she envelops me. The embrace is awkward because I'm still wearing my helmet and protective vest. I have to turn my head sideways to stop the helmet brim catching her in the chest. She clutches at the vest and squeezes me. This equipment is designed to save my life in the event of a fall, but it's no help at all in dealing with my mom. "You said it was too scary to watch."

"I know. But I decided I wouldn't be modeling good parental behaviour if I didn't support my daughter's athletic ambitions."

I'm used to this kind of comment because my mom is a psychologist with a counselling practice, and she often talks as though she expects her patients to be lurking behind trees, watching for inconsistencies between her actions and her advice to them. But I'm stunned when she goes on to say, "Besides, one of the other moms gave me a shot of scotch. I didn't even know people used hip flasks anymore. And then I waited in the car until I was sure it was all over. Are you okay?" She pushes me away and holds me at arm's length where she can scrutinize me for stress fractures, concussion, a post-trauma reaction, or any of the other things she always worries about.

"I'm fine. I'm great actually. We went clear. Even the ditch jump at number five, the one I was scared he would fall into—"

"No, stop, I don't want to hear about that," she says, letting me go. "Tell your father. He'll be back soon, he walked up to the last fence to take some video with his new camera."

"His camera does video?" My perfect day is turning into a potential total disaster. If Dad uploads the video footage to YouTube, I will never live it down. If Taylor sees it she will undertake a personal mission to convert me to her path of spiritual horsemanship. She will be sweetly relentless. There will be no more galloping, no jumping ginormous fences, no competitions. My days of having fun will be over. I so wish this was a dream.

"We're incredibly proud of you, Sweetie," says Mom, her arms swallowing me in another hug. I'm too tired and depressed to resist her. I can feel my champion self dissolving as I'm sucked back into my old life as an over-protected little alien nobody lost in a sea of humans. I'm half-smothered and about to lose consciousness when a desperate thought occurs to me: perhaps my dad doesn't know about YouTube. Maybe I'm getting ahead of myself here and nothing bad is going to happen. Maybe I can do something, delete the images, break the camera, something, anything, before he puts it where Taylor can find it. It's a slim hope, but enough to cling to.

"Mom, I can't breathe." I slide my arms between us and push myself free.

"Sorry, Honey," says Mom. Her fingers ring my upper arm. "You're getting so strong! Feel that muscle in there!"

"Thanks, Mom." I might be happier if I didn't know exactly where this was going.

"Think how much stronger you would be if you started your estrogen treatment."

"Not now, Mom."

"I know, I know. I'm leaving it to you. I'm just reminding, that's all."

I rip my arm away. I am an athlete, I remind myself, a successful one, in a high-risk sport. I stride off to find my horse.

Chapter Two

Mom and Dad have finished their dinner by the time I arrive home. Mom has saved mine in the fridge. She wants to warm it up, but I'm famished so eat it as is, cool, out of the storage container. Pasta with tuna, fennel and lemon. It's always good, but I'm so hungry it tastes like the best thing I've eaten in my life.

"Don't bolt your food, Pumpkin," says Mom.

I still haven't had a chance to tell anyone all about the jump course. I know my mom's not really interested, but I'm hoping if I downplay the scary bits she won't mind listening. "The first obstacle was pretty straightforward, a brush jump, but you know how Brooklyn likes to leap those like they're tall buildings. Number two was fun because there was a little corner so I had to pick our spot carefully and Brooklyn listened to me and we jumped it perfectly just like I'd planned, and then number three—"

"Slow down, Honey. Do you want dessert? I made blackberry apple cobbler, you can have it with ice cream if you like. Your father's finishing his now in the family room, you can join him there. He's doing something with his camera."

The camera. How could I have forgotten?

Mom loads up a bowl full of cobbler for me with more ice cream than I'm usually allowed. "Wow," I say. "Thanks, Mom."

"Well, you deserve it. You worked hard today and we're extremely proud of you. You're developing into quite the young lady."

My happy look freezes on my face.

"I'm not saying anything," says Mom, noticing the sudden chill in the air. "I'm not hinting. My lips are sealed on that front." She mimes a zipper closing across her mouth. As if that was possible. "Now, go look at your photos."

I take my dessert bowl into the family room. Maybe I can spill a little ice cream on the camera.

Dad is hunched over the computer keyboard. On the screen is a photo of me and Brooklyn in the starting box. We look fantastic. I was terrified, but in the photo I look intense and exhilarated. Brooklyn looks exactly the way he felt to me: barely containing his energy and raring to go.

There's no sign of the video footage.

"Hey, Dad," I say in a friendly semi-interested way.

"Oh, hey, Syl," says Dad. He stabs the Esc key three times. "Shit."

"Tony!" says Mom from the kitchen.

"Double shit," says Dad, whispering this time. "I can download the photos just fine, but damned if I can get that video clip." He's not speaking to me. He's just talking out loud.

But still, this is great. I wonder if I can leave him to screw it up all by himself, or not. Maybe not. He could figure it out. He might get desperate and refer to the user manual, which would not be good.

"Can I help?" I swirl my spoon in the ice cream, hoping to make it into a nice easily spillable consistency.

"What?" asks Dad, as though he's surprised I'm still here. He glances briefly in my direction before refocusing on the screen. "No, no thanks, Syl. What's this? Oh, there's a help menu."

Darn. Not good. I move closer to him as he scrolls through the help options. The camera is lying on the desk plugged into the computer keyboard. Slowly I lean on his shoulder, holding my bowl in my left hand over top of the camera, tilting it ever so slightly. A blackberry surfaces in the melted ice cream, floats over to the edge and bobbles promisingly.

"Aha. Here we go," says Dad, hitting a few more keys with his index finger. "Sound on."

Over the speakers I hear the rhythmic thumping of Brooklyn's hooves coming up the hill, and the sound of him breathing. I'm transported back to the moment, I know exactly how this felt and sounded and smelled, but from a totally different angle. On the screen the image of my panic-stricken face is obscured by the brim of my helmet, but I watch the desperate pull on the left rein, which Brooklyn ignores as the jump is fully in his sight. He is going very, very fast. And then he takes off a full stride before the jump. There's the faint thud of his feet hitting the log, not as loud as I heard it originally. He lands on the other side and immediately goes to his knees. My form is spectacular. I am upright and balanced and not interfering with his recovery in any way. He scrambles to his feet and canters on down the hill, reins flapping until I pick them up. The crowd cheers. They cheered for me! I didn't hear that before.

My dad's voice booms through the speaker, "That's my little girl! That's my girl up there! Hot damn is she good or what!" And then there's several scenes of grass and people's feet and sky and Dad's chin so I guess he was too excited to remember to turn off the camera. I've never heard him so proud. There's a huge burning lump in my throat.

"Great little camera, eh Syl?" says Dad, swivelling his chair to face me.

I'm taken off guard. My vision is blurry and out of nowhere I'm so tired from everything that's happened today that when he bumps me with his knees I automatically grab the dessert bowl with both hands and then fall back on my bum. Dad reaches a protective hand to the camera. The bowl slips from my grasp when I hit the floor and explodes at his feet.

"That was close!" he says, rolling out of the way. He bellows for my mom. "Evelyn! Bring some paper towels, would you?" He considers the growing oozing jagged puddle on the floor. "Jeez, Sylvie," he starts, but then he notices my face. "Oh look, it's just ice cream. It was an accident, nothing to cry about."

"Oh, Sylvie," says Mom, arriving with the paper towels. "What a mess."

"I bumped her," says Dad, suddenly prepared to acknowledge his part, even though he wasn't five seconds ago.

"It was one of the good bowls," says Mom. "From my mother's set." She sighs. "Oh well. What's done is done. That's probably what she would have said."

"No sense crying over spilled milk. Or ice cream. Right?" Dad laughs at his own joke, as usual.

I should stand up, but I can't. I should help to clean the floor, but I can't. I'd only be in the way.

"Ev, you missed some over there," says Dad, pointing.

"Sylvie, why don't you fetch us a washcloth and a bucket of warm soapy water from the kitchen?" asks Mom.

I wipe my face on my sleeve and slowly clamber to my feet. My bum is sore. Muscles all over the place are sore. I had a total workout today and only now am I noticing. I'd love a hot bath.

I pour some warm water and dish detergent into a bucket, grab a cloth and heft it all back to the family room.

"Wipe here," says Mom, as though I wouldn't know, as though I couldn't tell.

Dad rolls his chair out of the way and takes Mom by the elbow and stands her in front of the computer screen. "Here, Ev, look at this. That camera is fantastic, I can't believe I got 4K video for what I paid. I practically stole it." He fiddles with the keyboard, and I don't watch but again I hear the hoof beats, the breathing, the low thud, the cheering.

"Oh, good lord," says Mom. "Was that supposed to happen? Can horses do that—go to their knees and get up? It looked like he was going to somersault."

"Here, let me play it again on slow motion," says Dad. "This is such a cool feature."

"I can't watch," says Mom. "Once was enough." She stares at me, arms folded across her chest. "I don't know about this sport, Sylvie. I don't think a helmet and protective vest could save you from being crushed under a flipping horse."

"He didn't flip, Mom. He didn't even technically fall, because his shoulder and hindquarters didn't touch the ground." I wipe the floor again even though it's clean enough already.

"Don't imagine that you can distract me with technicalities," says Mom.

"I think I got it all here—the floor's clean," I say. "I'm sorry about Grandma's bowl."

"We'll be talking about this some more," says Mom. "Won't we, Tony?"

This is plenty bad enough, so I'm pretty well emotionally finished even before Dad chimes in with his announcement, "Uploading to YouTube—now!"

"Dad, no. I don't want you to. Please."

"Aw come on, Munchkin. Be proud. Promote yourself. You rode that like a pro." He isn't looking at me; his focus is fixed on the screen and progress updates from YouTube. There's no point in protesting.

I drop the cloth in the bucket. "I think I'll have a bath and go to bed. I'm really tired."

Mom picks up the bucket and takes it to the kitchen without saying another word, which says a lot.

"Don't worry, Syl," says Dad. "I'll send links to the family so you won't have to feel like you're bragging. Your Grandpa will like it. And Auntie Sally. And Taylor, of course. And the members of my photography club." He has opened a fresh email page and is composing as he talks. He is unstoppable.

I head to the bathroom for a soak. With a bit of luck, I'll drown and avoid all the trouble I'm otherwise heading for.

Chapter Three

I feel better in the morning, partly because I slept like a dead dog, and also because I had one of my lucid dreams, the ones where I know I'm dreaming and can control what happens. Sometimes I fly. Sometimes I meet up with Logan Losino. This time I retrace every stride of the cross-country course. It's almost as good as talking to someone about it. The best part is, when Brooklyn and I are approaching that last jump, I'm able to slow him down. He approaches in a balanced canter, takes off at the perfect spot, leaps in a rounded bascule, lands, doesn't fall to his knees, and canters to the finish line where everyone is cheering.

When I climb out of bed, I notice even more sore muscles than last night. Yesterday was quite the workout. And, I have to admit, it was also quite the accomplishment, no matter what the fallout might be. I completed a one-day three-phase event including a cross-country course, which has been a lifelong ambition. It was scary and difficult and I did it. *We* did it, me and Brooklyn. I couldn't care less about ribbons or trophies. I'm proud of both of us.

I poke through my dresser looking for something suitable to wear to school—clothes that show I am strong and athletic and not to be messed with. There's nothing like that in my wardrobe. I am almost fifteen, but my clothes are all designed to fit an undeveloped eight-year-old, because I have Turner Syndrome. I will never be taller than four feet, ten inches, and I will not develop unless I take estrogen. There is a box full of estrogen patches in the back right corner of my top drawer. I see it has been moved from where I carefully placed it. Mom's been snooping again. Well, I won't be starting estrogen today, that's for sure. Today I want to enjoy the pure satisfaction of my success as an athlete. I'm not interested in the complications and developments that will come with a surge of hormones. I've only just arrived as this new triumphant me—why would I change now? I re-adjust the position of the box so it is again not quite in the corner of the drawer, then drape a pair of socks over the edge so I'll know if Mom comes back on another espionage mission.

What I'd really like to wear today is kick-ass black jeans and a black t-shirt, but of course I don't have those. I settle for the least pastel shades I can find, which means blue jeans and a purple and green checked shirt that Kansas found for me during one of her regular visits to the hospital thrift store.

I open my email before breakfast. There are two messages from Taylor. Each has a link along with the same brief note: "Hi Sylvia. Read this. Love, Taylor." The first link goes to an article in *Horse and Hound* about some eventer who died in Germany in a rotational fall. What is a rotational fall and why should I care? I decide not to read it. The second is about how to be your horse's best friend. I decide not to read that one either. I already am Brooklyn's best friend.

Mom and Dad are waiting for me at the breakfast table.

I feel the aura of the United Front Technique as soon as I step in the kitchen. I shove my hands deep in my pockets. Don't mess with me, I say to myself. I have faced danger before.

"Your father and I have been talking about that video," says Mom.

I lean nonchalantly against the refrigerator instead of grabbing a bowl and the box of Shreddies as I would normally do. Dad is fidgeting and taking sneak peeks at his watch. Usually he's out the door to a meeting by now. Mom has a more leisurely schedule on Mondays because her eating disorders group doesn't start until ten. Still, I know the warning signs and symptoms will be on her mind so she should be easily knocked off course.

"We're all in support of you pursuing athletic activities," says Mom, pouring herself a coffee. "But as parents we have to make judgment calls about sports that might have long-term health consequences."

Yeah, yeah, yeah. You're not talking me out of this one. Not that I'm stupid enough to say so out loud. I reach toward my jacket hanging on the back of my kitchen chair.

"Are you leaving without having breakfast?" says Mom.

"I'm not hungry," I say even though I'm starving. "And I'm in training. It would be good to reduce my carbs. I think I'm looking chubby. I want to be more lean." I hope I haven't overdone it—I know I've used multiple trigger words and Dad is considering me suspiciously over the top of his glasses.

"Oh Sweetie, you are not chubby. And you have to eat breakfast. Your brain doesn't work properly without food. People who don't eat breakfast have less mental clarity compared to people who regularly eat a healthy breakfast," says Professor Mom.

I am fortunate that she is easily distracted.

"Maybe I'll have a little," I say. I pour myself a quarter of my usual serving.

"More than that, for heaven's sake, Cupcake," says Mom.

I top up the bowl, add a drop of milk and sigh heavily as I take a seat at the table. Dad's eyebrows are vibrating from his desperation to bolt out the door. I casually glance at my watch. "Oh wow. Is it eight o'clock already?"

Dad's fingers drum the table top in a sharp staccato. This won't take long. I stir my cereal and slowly eat one square.

"Are you feeling okay, Sylvie?" says Mom. She pats my forehead, checking for fever.

"I'm tired. Athletes often require a recovery day."

"You're not thinking of missing school?"

"Oh no, of course not."

"Fine then," says Mom.

Dad takes this as his cue. "Fine," he says. He launches from his chair, grabs his jacket, kisses Mom on the cheek, tousles my head like I'm a golden retriever, opens the door and escapes before Mom can say a peep.

Mom brings her coffee to the table and takes a seat. I thought she was done, but apparently there's more to come. Oh well. I pour on extra milk and set to devouring my cereal. I will need my strength to deal with her, because I'm not about to give up riding or jumping or eventing—not in a million years.

"I didn't buy you that shirt, did I?" says Mom.

"Kansas gave it to me."

"Ah," says Mom. This has explained everything. "Are you really wearing it to school? It's not just the style... the collar is frayed."

"Mom. I'm not six."

She sips her coffee and grabs a banana from the fruit basket in the middle of the table.

"You call that a breakfast?" I say.

"I'm not six either, Sylvie."

I nod. Fair enough. In a way, I like this. The playing field has levelled. We are going to treat each other like adults. I relax a little.

But then Mom says, "Well, now that I've got you here, maybe this would be a good time for a woman-to-woman chat."

Oh no. I misread the play. Not that topic again. Alert! Alert!

"How's it going with the estrogen patches?"

I stand my spoon up straight in my bowl and stare at the handle. "Uh, fine?"

"Have you started using them?"

She knows I haven't. She's been checking. But I can't let her know that I know without revealing my secret sock booby trap. "Uh, not yet. But I'm thinking about it."

Mom returns the banana to the basket.

"Sylvie, you know I wouldn't normally intrude on your privacy but... "

She stops because I've let go of my spoon and it clanks against the edge of the bowl. Is she kidding? I check her face for signs of a joke, but her expression is unreadable. Is she lying or can she have no idea how intrusive she is all the time?

"... but your health is at stake," she finishes.

"Mom, I know. We've been through all this. I'm going to start, but not today."

"You've been saying that for weeks, Sylvie."

I hate it when she pushes me, even if she's right. "Mom, you said I could decide for myself when I wanted to start."

"You won't develop unless you use the patches, Pumpkin."

A great heat surges up my back and over the top of my head. My pulse is pounding and I am suddenly so enraged I can't control myself. "I know that," I shout at her. "But for once I would like to be in charge of me. Even the doctor said the timing was up to me. The more you push, the less I know if I'm ready."

Mom's fingers encircle her coffee mug. "There's no need to lose your temper, Sylvie," she says flatly.

"Yes, there is. Because otherwise you don't listen to me. You keep at me and at me until I can't think or breathe." Mom shakes her head and opens her mouth but I cut her off before she can say anything. "Mom, if you bring this up one more time, I will take that box of patches and throw them in the garbage. If you so much as hint, they will be gone, and I will never develop into a young woman, I will stay forever exactly the way I am and that will be fine with me." Even as I say this, I know it isn't true. If she accuses me of bluffing, I'll be finished.

But she doesn't. She quietly considers the coffee vibrating in her mug. A heavy silence permeates the kitchen. Outside, sparrows are chirping in the hedge and someone across the street starts a lawnmower. Out there, life goes on, while in here my sexual development hangs in the balance.

Mom nods her head. "I promise," she says.

Chapter Four

Victorious on two fronts (as an athlete and a self-directed human being) I arrive at school expecting to continue the trend. I'm hoping to see Logan Losino as soon as possible and give him a jump-by-jump account of my triumph on the cross-country course. Instead I am met at the front door by Amber and Topaz, the Tormenting Twins.

"Hey, Cowgirl," says Amber. Topaz grins vacantly behind her. "Nice rodeo outfit you're wearing. You planning on doing some lamb-wrestling? Because we all know you're too teensy to handle a steer."

She is such an idiot.

I have faced a drop fence, a double oxer and a coffin jump. I have subdued my mother in an argument. I can do anything. Except, apparently, think of an appropriate sassy response to Amber. I duck under her arm and march in the direction of my locker.

She follows, flapping at me with her notebook. When this fails to provoke a response from me, she starts bah-ing wildly, like a sheep having a panic attack. When I arrive at my locker, Amber reaches over me and holds it closed with one hand. As much as I tug on the handle I can't budge her. So much for being a successful athlete. I am still a midget.

"I hope you're not late for class," says Amber. "I hope you don't get a detention or get put back a grade or two to where you belong with the other infant-sized children."

I guess I'm too tired. My muscles are sore, I'm supposed to be having a recovery day, and instead I've had a confrontation with my mom and now this. I can't think of anything to say. I look at her hand lying flat on my locker in front of my face. I could bite it, right there where her thumb meets her wrist. I'd probably draw blood. I'd have Amber's blood in my mouth. That would be awful, but it might shut her up.

Though she could have AIDS because her boyfriend Franco is a notorious hound dog, so I should avoid contact with her blood. I should. But it is so tempting. I can see the pulse throbbing in her wrist. One chomp. I prepare to lunge.

"Hey, what's going on here? Am I missing something?" Logan Losino has come to my rescue, as he always does. I swear he has a sixth sense about when I need protection.

"Just the usual," says Topaz, yawning.

"Oh, it's little Logan," says Amber. Relations between Logan and Amber have deteriorated since Amber started dating Franco. Logan is Franco's younger brother and Amber used to make a huge fuss over him. Now that she's moved on to an older Losino, she acts like she's even more special and Logan is nothing. Logan has told me this doesn't bother him. He's more troubled by what's happening at home because Amber encourages Franco's natural bullying tendencies.

"Hey Amber. Are you seeing Francopithecus after school?" says Logan.

"Franco what?" asks Amber. "Are you being disrespectful? Because he won't like that."

"It's his family nickname, Amber. We're always joking around at our house." That's partially true. Logan and his dad are complete jokesters. I wouldn't say the same about Franco.

"No way," says Topaz.

"A nickname?" asks Amber. Like Franco, she's not endowed with much of a sense of humour. Her endowments are more of the physical variety. She flaunts them now, bouncing in front of Logan's face. She is disgusting.

"Right—it's Latin," says Logan, ripping his eyes away. "You can try it on him some time if you need to make him laugh. Here, let me spell it for you." He slips a pen out of his pocket and prints *FRANCOPITHECUS* on the inside front page of Amber's notebook. It's Latin all right, for big hairy apelike creature.

Amber reads it silently, lips moving. "How do you pronounce it again? I'll never get it right."

"I'll help you," says Topaz, taking her by the arm and walking her away. "Franc-o-pith-a-cuss."

I open my locker and stash my jacket. "Thanks, Logan."

"No problem."

"He'll kill her if she calls him that."

Logan shrugs. "Amber is indestructible. How was your weekend?"

Oh. He asked. Someone actually asked. And in the ten minutes remaining before class I tell him about the cross-country, jump by freaking jump. And he listens, and doesn't change the subject, and only interrupts to get more information, like, "Exactly what is a coffin jump?" And when I finally finish (without mentioning the time penalty points) I'm just as excited and happy as I was when I rode the course, and then Logan says, "That sounds awesome. You are amazing," and I didn't think I could possibly feel better than yesterday, but I do, I truly do.

Chapter Five

During lunch break, I'm looking for some peace and quiet and instead I stumble upon Taylor in the library. She's tucked away in a study carrel, drawing pictures of Spike in her Aboriginal Studies notebook.

I might as well talk to her. Taylor is my second-best friend, after Brooklyn, and I don't exactly have a huge pool of pals to take her place.

I tap her on the shoulder.

"Oh. It's you," she says. She returns to her drawing, adding a cloud of hearts above Spike's head. "Horses are all about love," she murmurs. This is easy for Taylor to say because she never rides. She owns Spike who is a hinny, a cross between a male donkey and a female horse. She says she refuses to treat him like a beast of burden, so they do other things instead, such as taking long walks side by side on the forest trails practicing psychic bonding. She's trying to coordinate their breathing and heart-rate patterns. No kidding. Boring or what?

"Are you going to the barn after school? I thought maybe we could do the trails together."

"I don't think so," says Taylor.

"I could walk. I don't have to ride." I can't believe I've suggested this.

"I'm surprised you're allowed to ride. If Kansas had any sense she'd ground you. Though in a way, I suppose she's part of the problem, being so mainstream about horse training." She closes her notebook and looks behind me, scanning the library for more acceptable company, an angel perhaps, or an international horse whisperer.

"Brooklyn likes me riding him. He likes jumping. He likes going fast. What is the problem?"

"You are responsible for him, Sylvia. He could have broken his legs at that last jump. Or he could have flipped and crushed you to death. Did you not read that article on rotational falls?"

"But he didn't!" This is so frustrating. "And everyone knows that eventing is a dangerous sport."

"Brooklyn doesn't know. You have to take care of him. Sometimes you can't let him do what he wants to do. He doesn't know he could break a leg. Horses live in the moment."

Oh, here we go again.

"Please don't look at me like that," says Taylor.

"Like what? I wasn't doing anything."

"I know what you're thinking." She thinks she's a mind reader, just like my mom.

"I'm not thinking anything!"

"My point precisely," says Taylor. "And you better not be expecting me to help you at your next event either, because I'm not."

"Fine then," I say. "I'll see you around."

I leave her there before she can tell me anything else I don't need to hear. It's not as though I'm abusive. I love Brooklyn. I tell him everything. I spend every spare minute I can with him. So what if I break one little rule at one cross-country event. Nothing bad happened. We're talking grass-stained knees, that's all. Taylor should cut me some slack.

I wander around, hoping to run into Logan Losino, but can't find him anywhere.

I'm alone, cut from the herd.

I try to stop my thoughts but it's too late. A-L-O-N-E. My palms break into a sweat and my heart takes off pounding in my chest like a trapped rabbit. I hate hate hate it when this happens. I know I'm not the first person people want to have as a friend. I know I look unusual. I understand, but it doesn't help. I've been dealing with being unusual ever since everyone else started to grow and I didn't. You'd think I'd be used to it by now, but instead I feel flat-out panicked as every past episode of being teased or shunned floods into my brain.

I stop at a water fountain for a drink. I let the cool water splash over my cheeks. I wipe my face on my sleeve and concentrate on steadying my breathing. In-two-three-four-out-two-three-four. I'm okay. There's no sabre-toothed tiger. There's just kids, like me... well, not exactly like me, no one's like me, I am a singularity, an oddball, a misfit. In-two-three-four-out-two-three-four. I need to get out of here. I stare down the bank of lockers towards the corner that leads to the cafeteria. Right foot, left foot, look calm and confident and no one will pick on me. I don't feel ready for a crowd of people, but maybe Logan will be there, finishing his lunch. I'm desperate to see someone who likes me. Right left, breathe in out, right left. Off I go.

I am concentrating on my feet, left right left, and

rounding the corner, I bump full into Topaz. Automatically I turn to head off in the other direction.

"Hey, Sylvia. How's things?"

I stop in my tracks. Is Topaz being nice to me? Is this possible? I turn slowly and check to see if Amber is lurking behind her. Amber is the real troublemaker. Topaz mostly follows her lead. Sometimes when Topaz is on her own she's almost friendly. "Fine. I guess."

"You don't look so fine. Your face is like a beet, and your hair... "

"I'm fine."

"You look upset."

And you care? Maybe she does. She looks like she cares. Her head is tilted to one side and she's frowning.

"It's no big deal," I say. "Taylor's disappointed in me, that's all."

"Yeah well, Amber's going to be disappointed with me, and that's a huge deal." She leans her back against a locker and slides her bum to the floor. I look down at the top of her head. Her hair is a mess. From my usual angle of at least a foot shorter than everybody, I never get to see this.

"We're not supposed to sit in the hallway," I say.

She hugs her knees to her chest. "I don't care. Maybe I'll get expelled and then I can go to another school where Amber and Franco won't follow me."

"There is no other school."

"Maybe I'll do home-schooling."

"How would that keep you away from Amber?"

"Oh, never mind," she says. She bangs her forehead against her knees.

I don't know what to do. I can't leave her there, not when she's being friendly to me. I touch her foot with the end of my sneaker.

"So now you're kicking me?" she says. At least she stops the head banging.

"I'm not kicking. I'm nudging."

"Well, stop it."

Now she doesn't seem so friendly. This is confusing. And even if I wanted to help her, I wouldn't know what to say. Though perhaps that is a good place to start. "I don't know how to fix my own problems, so how can I help you with yours?"

"Good point," says Topaz.

Mom would give me a cup of tea if she was trying to help me. I wish I had something to give Topaz, like a Coke, or a stick of gum, or a bag of chips. Or a hairbrush.

"Do you still own a horse?" asks Topaz.

"Yes."

"I wish I had a horse, instead of a twin."

"Horses can cause problems too," I say.

She laughs. "No horse in the world could cause more problems than Amber."

"I'll agree with you there," I say.

Topaz relaxes her grip on her knees and stretches her legs out into the hallway. She looks up at me, squinting. "So what exactly is wrong with you?" she says.

"Like I said, Taylor's upset with me, so I'm feeling—"

"No, not that. What's *wrong* with you? Logan says we're supposed to be nice to you because you're handicapped or something."

Logan Losino thinks I'm *handicapped?* I feel like my chest has been pierced with a lance. How could he think such a thing? And even if he thought it, how could he tell my enemies? Or is Topaz making this up? I nudge her foot again. Okay, this time it is more of a kick. "I'm missing a chromosome, that's all. It's called Turner Syndrome. I am not handicapped."

"But you're really short."

"Lots of people are short. That doesn't make it a handicap. Geez. Lots of people are stupid. They're not handicapped."

Topaz twiddles her hair with her fingers. One of the frizzy clumps falls to the side revealing a bald patch the size of an egg. The hair around it is sparse, like my dad's. I'm tempted to touch it. I'm wondering if there's a lump underneath like when the young deer grow antlers and this small bulge starts on their skull. Then again, maybe she has some sort of contagious skin condition, so touching wouldn't be such a great idea.

Topaz says, "Missing a chromosome sounds like a major problem. I mean, you can't fix it, can you? What happens to you? Will you ever grow up?"

"I probably won't get any taller, if that's what you mean. If I take estrogen supplements I'll develop like other girls." Usually I don't talk about Turners—it's too personal. I'm halfways disgusted with myself for talking to Topaz, as if I'm so desperate for a friend I'll say anything. But at the same time I'm surprised to find that talking about Turners with someone who doesn't have a big emotional investment in it (like my Mom, for one humungous example) actually feels pretty good. It's like a weight comes off my shoulders. Weird.

Topaz pulls a single hair out of the top of her head and examines it closely. "So you're telling me that without supplements you won't develop?"

"Right," I say.

"Which means you have a choice. You can have cramps and periods and accidents and stinky sweat and mood swings and harassment from boys who are only interested in your body... or not."

I can't believe she's got it. My sworn enemy seems to understand something better than my own mother. Or half of it anyway.

"On the other hand, it would be good to be normal like everyone else," I say.

"Well, I know what I'd choose," says Topaz. "Normal is over-rated. It would be way easier to be a freak."

I swing my leg and kick her foot really hard. I don't think about it, I just do it. Topaz screams and scrambles to her feet, and she's probably going to kill me but that's when Mr. Brumby arrives and marches us both to the office.

Fighting in the hallway. Me. I can't believe it. I am not a violent person. Or I don't think I am. Maybe I don't know myself as well as I think I do. I could be a violent freaky handicapped animal abuser who's in denial.

Chapter Six

Mr. Brumby points to a row of grey plastic chairs that would not look out of place in a prison. "Sit there while I sort this out."

I take a seat at one end and Topaz takes one at the other. I swing my legs in what I hope will appear to be a confident carefree manner. I do not look at Topaz, the troublemaking creep. I have never been sent to the principal's office in my life, and I am offended and frightened. Fortunately I have faced danger before.

Mr. Brumby forges ahead to the desk of Mrs. Cobb, the office secretary. She makes him wait until she has closed several screens on her computer. He crosses his arms and taps a foot.

"Yes, Mr. Brumby?"

"These two were scrapping in the hallway," he says, gesturing with his chin in our direction.

Mrs. Cobb slides her glasses into place at the top of her nose and considers us skeptically. "These two?"

"That's what I said." Mr. Brumby is not accustomed to being questioned. He teaches math, and rules with an iron hand. My mom says he is missing a basic understanding of human motivation, but that I am to treat him with respect regardless—as if I would dare show disrespect to someone who is always looking like he's on the verge of blowing an aneurysm.

"Unfortunately, Mr. Brumby, the Principal is in meetings all afternoon. Just a minute." Mrs. Cobb picks up her phone and says, "Can you hold please?" She presses a button and places the phone back in its cradle.

Mr. Brumby has been shifting his weight from one foot to another and now re-crosses his arms.

"I don't know what you want me to do, Mr. Brumby. You can't leave them here with me, I'm not authorized."

"Then the school counsellor will have to deal with them." He points to the closed door of Ms. Teke's office.

"Ms. Teke is away sick," says Mrs. Cobb.

"Away sick?" shouts Mr. Brumby.

"No doubt she's sorry she didn't clear it with you first," says Mrs. Cobb. She takes a key from her drawer and unlocks Ms. Teke's door. "She won't mind you using her office, Mr. Brumby, as long as you don't disturb anything. I have to take that call." She returns to her desk and picks up the phone. "Sorry for the delay. Can I help you now?" She turns her back to Mr. Brumby. There's no other way to break his evil stare. He glares at her head for about thirty seconds. Anyone else would have melted into their chair, but Mrs. Cobb carries on a cheery conversation about parking space allocation.

I'm hoping Mr. Brumby will let us go. I sneak a look in Topaz's direction. She has her hands in a prayer position and mouths the word *Please!*

Mr. Brumby raps a knuckle on Mrs. Cobb's desk, which

she ignores, and eventually he swings around to look at me and Topaz.

"All right, you two. Into the office. What are you waiting for?"

I bolt in ahead of Topaz. Mr. Brumby follows and half closes the door behind him. I see Mrs. Cobb cover the mouthpiece of the phone; she swivels in her chair and says, "Remember, Mr. Brumby, this school has zero tolerance for violence or bullying."

For an instant I'm relieved that she has reminded him, and that he will be gentler with us, but then I realize she wasn't referring to his behaviour, she meant me and Topaz. Zero tolerance. I am going to be expelled. How will I explain this to my parents? They will never forgive me. Their plans for me include university, and now I'm not going to make my way out of high school.

Mr. Brumby uses his foot to push the door so it's not exactly closed, but the opening is too small for Mrs. Cobb to see through. We are at his mercy. He's frightening enough when he's frustrated during math class and there are more than twenty of us to dilute his wrath.

Ms. Teke has arranged her office with the desk against the wall and five chairs in a cozy sharing circle. There's nowhere to hide.

Mr. Brumby clears his throat and tells us to sit, so of course we do, like obedient puppies. I don't like being in this small a room with Mr. Brumby. He takes up too much space, or air, or subatomic energy. I can hardly breathe.

Mr. Brumby ignores us as he nudges the books in the bookcase so the spines all line up evenly with the edge of the shelf. He picks up the framed photo of a black cocker spaniel from Ms. Teke's desk, and puts it down, placing it precisely on the corner so it becomes the hypotenuse of an equilateral triangle.

He must be employing a delaying technique to instill fear and obedience. If he carries on like this for much longer, I'll admit to anything.

Finally he turns around, and at first I'm afraid to look at his face. If it's red and blotchy, we're dead.

But I have faced danger before. I make myself look up at him. He seems strangely calm. He reaches for the sweater that Ms. Teke has left looped over the back of one of the remaining chairs. If his face was blotchy, I'm sure he would tear the sweater to pieces and toss it in the trashcan, but instead he folds it in half, and then in half again, and I'm expecting he's going to attempt one more fold to create a perfectly symmetrical little package, when he raises the sweater to his nose and— I can't believe my eyes. He sniffs her sweater. What is that about? He's quick about it, but I know he did it, just before dropping the sweater on an empty seat and giving it a gentle pat.

Topaz has missed this bizarre behaviour, she is too busy twiddling her hair and reading the motivational posters on the wall, ones about having a positive attitude and about how every day is special and how *anger* is one letter short of *danger*.

Mr. Brumby doesn't sit down. He tilts a chair onto its hind legs and leans on it, all the better to loom over us.

"I'm surprised at you, Sylvia," he says.

I could say the same to him. I look from Mr. Brumby to the sweater and back again.

Mr. Brumby raises a single finger to his lips and shakes his head. Is this a message? What is he saying?

"I wasn't bullying anybody," says Topaz, breaking into our silent conversation. "She kicked me."

"She called me a freak," I explain.

"I did not," says Topaz.

"Which is ironic if you think about it, coming from someone who's going bald." I know this is mean, and I wouldn't have said it if she hadn't lied.

Topaz slaps both hands on top of her head and looks at me with huge wet eyes. "I am not going bald," she says.

"I am not a freak," I say. "And I'm not handicapped either."

"All right, that's enough," says Mr. Brumby. "I have the picture." The sweater takes his attention again. His face softens, like he's in a trance. The sweater has put him under a spell. How weird is that?

Maybe I won't be expelled after all.

Mr. Brumby takes a seat and clears his throat. "Obviously, this is not my area," he says. No kidding. "How do you think Ms. Teke would deal with this problem, Sylvia?"

"I have no idea," I say. "I'm never in trouble. Ask Topaz."

"I'm never in trouble either," says Topaz. "Maybe we should go find Amber and Franco. They have lots of experience with this sort of thing."

And I don't mean to, but somehow this makes me laugh.

Topaz snickers and Mr. Brumby glares at her briefly, but then his eyes flick to the anger/danger poster.

"Well, you have put things in perspective, Topaz," says Mr. Brumby. "You two aren't what I would call habitual troublemakers." He points to the clock on the wall. "Lunch break is almost over. If you want to avoid detentions, we'll have to resolve this quickly. So what do we do?"

"We'll promise to behave more appropriately," I say. Topaz nods with enthusiasm.

Mr. Brumby slaps his thighs and stands. "That will do for me." I can't believe he bought this. Mr. Brumby is hardcore, and to have accepted this bit of fluffiness is completely out of character. "Off you go then," he says, pointing to the door.

Topaz rushes away like her shoes have caught fire. I'm halfway to the door when Mr. Brumby asks me to wait.

"We all have lives outside of school," he says.

"Okay," I say, but I'm doubtful. I know that I have a life outside of school, but I can't imagine Mr. Brumby having one.

"All of us," insists Mr. Brumby. "And the outside lives can be kept separate. Right, Pipsqueak?"

Pipsqueak. He called me *Pipsqueak.* I've been trying to be pleasant and cooperative and he calls me that? I know I'm short, but he doesn't have to rub my nose in it. What a jerk.

"Wait a minute," he says, reading my face. "No, Sylvia—"

I stomp out of the office and slam the door behind me. Mrs. Cobb shakes her head as I pass. "How can a math teacher not understand the zero in *zero tolerance*?" she says.

I don't know when I've been more humiliated. Mr. Brumby was completely inappropriate. I'll tell my mom and probably she can have him fired. Except that there were no witnesses; it would be my word against his, and I know how that would turn out.

I storm past Topaz. "Where you going?" she says, grabbing my arm. "What's the matter? I thought everything turned out great."

Now she wants to be friends again? This is driving me crazy. I might have broken free if her reinforcements hadn't arrived.

"Topaz, I've been looking for you everywhere," says Amber.

Topaz twiddles her hair. "Not everywhere. "

"Stop doing that," says Amber, batting at her hand.

Topaz puts both hands behind her back and glowers at Amber.

"I wish I had a special-needs friend," says Amber, glancing

in my direction. "Will you share, Topaz?" She turns and smiles at me with all the warmth of the Wicked Witch of the West.

"At least I have a functioning heart," I say.

She takes a menacing step in my direction. "What did you say, Pigmy Chimp?"

Topaz slides into her path, grabs her arm and swings her down the hall. "Brumby just about gave me a detention, but I talked my way out of it," she says, taking all the credit. Would a friend do that? I can't figure her out at all.

Amber laughs. "A detention? You broke a rule? Oh I'm so proud of you." She slips an arm around Topaz's shoulders, pulls her close and kisses her on the ear.

They totter away, together in their perfect if non-identical twinniness. I wonder what it would be like, to be that close to another human being, someone you've been together with since before you were born, sharing everything. I wonder how my life would have been different if I had had a twin. But I will never know. I don't even have a sister; all I have is my cousin Taylor. We probably wouldn't be friends if we weren't related, because we are not at all similar. I love her, but I don't understand her. And I suppose she would say the same about me, or at least she might have said so in the past, before I disappointed her so deeply.

I used to believe that Logan Losino understood me, but not now, not if he thinks I'm some sort of handicapped shrimp. Nobody gets me, except for Brooklyn. And me. I get me, I'm pretty sure I do. I take a deep steadying breath. I'm okay. All I have to do is survive until three o'clock, because then school will be over for the day and I can head to the barn. That's not such a big deal. Two hours. Anybody can do that.

Chapter Seven

Normally, the barn is my sanctuary. Life can be a total mess, but if I stand in the quiet of the barn, smelling the horses and the hay, sliding my fingers through Brooklyn's mane, listening to him chew... I know it's ridiculous, but all my troubles fade away. It doesn't matter that I'm short, that I am missing an x-chromosome, that I don't have friends, that my parents are both total nutbars. If I can hang out with Brooklyn, I am fine.

Not today.

Taylor arrived before me and has disappeared somewhere to commune with Spike, leaving her backpack hanging on Spike's stall door like a reminder of her absence from my life.

Kansas has still not forgiven me. She stomped past me down the alleyway while I was picking out Brooklyn's feet, and shut herself in the tack room. Obviously, there will be no riding lesson today. I thought school was bad, but this is worse because school is always bad so my expectations are low. I'd hoped better for my time at the barn. I feel disappointed on top of being depressed.

I spend more time than usual grooming Brooklyn, hoping that Kansas will exit the tack room so I can grab my saddle and bridle. Brooklyn is positively gleaming, every strand of mane and tail is soft and free, and there's not a speck of muck anywhere. Usually, I only fuss this much before a show, or when someone important is coming to visit, especially my grandpa because he was the one who found Brooklyn for me in the first place and shipped him out from Saskatchewan.

"What am I going to do?" I whisper to him. "If I go in the tack room I'll get lectured, whether I apologize or not." Brooklyn drops his head and uses his nose to investigate my pockets for carrots. I lean on his shoulder. "I guess we could just go for a walk."

I lead Brooklyn into the yard and let him take me wherever he wants, which is from one patch of untrimmed grass to another. Kansas's boyfriend, Declan, is on the roof of the house he is building beside the travel trailer that Kansas has been calling home since she set up the stable. He waves to me then returns to his hammer and nails.

Brooklyn and I end up against the back of the barn beneath the tack room window. Inside I can hear Kansas snuffling and blowing her nose as if she's having some sort of allergic reaction. She's never had allergies before. She gasps for breath. Will I need to call an ambulance? But then it dawns on me. She's crying. Have I upset her that much? Kansas never cries. She is cowgirl tough. Plus she's a boss mare. I feel terrible to have made her this sad. If it wasn't for Kansas, I wouldn't have learned to ride. If not for her, I would never have been able to follow my dreams. I have to do something.

"I'm fine," I hear her say. Now she's talking to herself. She's doing positive affirmations, like my mom is always telling me to do, only I'm supposed to be more specific:

I am beautiful, I am intelligent, I am perfect the way I am.
Kansas is being too vague. I could give her some advice on this.

Kansas speaks again. "No, no. It's the hormones, really." These can't be affirmations—she must be on her phone. She probably had to find a quiet place to talk, away from all the hammer noise. Of course, it's not right to eavesdrop, but if I'm the cause of her being so upset, listening would give me clues about what I should do to help.

"Everything's fine," says Kansas, sniffling loudly. Who does she think she's kidding? "Declan's working on the house, and it's going to be really nice." Her voice is about an octave higher than it's supposed to be, that's how hard she's trying not to break down. There's a long pause, then she says, "Mom, I know. But we'll be fine. I'll put Hambone on the market—he's never been much good as a lesson horse."

She's going to sell Hambone? She can't sell Hambone, he's the best horse she's ever had. It will break her heart!

"After the baby is born and we know exactly what we're dealing with, I'll start teaching again, and if Hambone's gone there will be a stall free so I can take in another boarder. Everything will be fine." Another pause, and she blows her nose. "Well, we'd love to see you, of course, but there's no room for you to stay here. The house is great, it's almost finished, but it's really tiny." Pause. "No, I mean really tiny." Pause. "I'm sure you could help, but—" The pitch of her voice is dropping. I know what that means. Now she's getting mad. "Well, it's too late for that now, isn't it? We made an informed choice, it may be difficult but we will manage. You need to back off, Mom." Oh boy, I can so identify with this, but at the same time I'm shocked that boss mare Kansas has had to deal with an interfering mother too. And apparently her mother is even more determined than mine, because Kansas raises the volume as she continues, "No... look, I've got to go, I have a lesson starting. Do not buy a bus ticket, you understand? We need to talk about this—I'll call you later."

I hear the tack room door open and slam shut, then Kansas is bellowing for me. We're having a lesson after all. I tug on the lead rope and drag Brooklyn's head out of the grass. "I'm not sure this is a good idea at all," I tell him. He stops and looks longingly at another patch of green. "Let's see if we can talk her out of it."

Kansas appears from around the corner of the barn. "Oh, there you are," she says with exaggerated happiness. Is this what people do when they want to hide how they're feeling? I'll have to remember next time I need space from my mom.

I look pointedly from her to the tack room window and back again.

"You were eavesdropping?"

"I didn't mean to. I was hand-grazing Brooklyn under the window."

Kansas sighs. "Oh well."

"Do you really want to teach today? You sound kind of upset."

She shrugs and sighs again, then sits on the bench outside the main door. I take a seat beside her. Brooklyn gives up on the idea of finding more grass, drops his head beside my shoulder and takes a nap.

Kansas considers Brooklyn. "I wish I could fall asleep that easily."

I don't know what to say. Kansas isn't as old as my parents, but she's an adult with adult problems and I'm just a kid.

"Are you really going to sell Hambone?"

Kansas nods. "This baby is going to be expensive."

"More than most babies?"

"Yes, more than most." Kansas reaches over and takes my free hand, the one not attached to Brooklyn's lead rope. This is very weird. Kansas is not a touchy-feely kind of person. The pregnancy hormones must have turned her brain to mush.

"I'm sorry I upset you by going too fast on the cross-country," I say.

Kansas takes in a jagged sniff, as though she's trying not to cry again.

"I'm really sorry. I won't do it again. Even though it was fun and Brooklyn liked galloping a lot. If it upsets you this much, it's not worth it."

"Oh, Sylvia," says Kansas, and then she moans.

She's breaking my heart. "I promise," I say. What else can I do?

Kansas shakes her head. "It's not that, Sylvia. There's something else. It's not about you... well, it is sort of about you, but it's not your fault, it's not what you think. Oh, damn," she says, and she drops my hand and levers herself to her feet. "Don't worry, I'll tell you another time. Go ride your horse, have some fun." And she waddles across the parking lot to her house.

Have some fun. Right. As though that is possible now.

Brooklyn takes a step closer to me. He's well into my personal zone, something Kansas doesn't approve of, she says it's dangerous and horses have to respect my space and not intrude unless invited. Brooklyn rests his muzzle on my head and wiggles his lips in my hair. He explores my ear, and blows into it, then he holds his nostril in front of my nose and I smell his sweet grassy breath. I watch the groove on his neck where his pulse is visible, showing his great generous heart throbbing slowly along. The tension flows out of me and all may not be right with the world, but I can manage, I truly can.

Chapter Eight

Mom is making chicken stir-fry for dinner. Whenever she cooks this meal, even though it's supposed to be quick and easy, she always looks frazzled. She says it's because of the high heat from the wok, and the exertion from chopping a mountain of vegetables, and the stress of delivering the finished product to the table at precisely the right time, not overcooked, not undercooked, and then there's the rice... I wish she'd just use frozen vegetables, but she says their nutritional content is not as high as fresh, and the least she can do is put a wholesome meal on the table for her family.

Given a choice, I'd rather have fewer nutrients and a calmer Mom.

My plan is to wait until we're partway through our meal, then ask Dad how Kansas can deal with her financial problems without selling Hambone. My dad is a financial planning professional; I know he'll have lots of ideas even though he's not Kansas's biggest fan because he doesn't cope well with boss mares. I'll have to plan my questions carefully, otherwise a conversation about horses is bound to turn into another lecture about the dangers of equestrian sports.

Mom tucks a loose strand of hair behind her ear as she examines her plate of food. "So tell me, Pumpkin," she says without looking at me, "were there any times you felt proud of yourself today?"

Proud of myself. I think back on my day, about Taylor trying to convince me how irresponsible I am, about learning that Logan Losino thinks I'm handicapped, about kicking Topaz for calling me a freak, about being in the office with Mr. Brumby, about eavesdropping on Kansas. What was there to be proud of in that mishmash?

My dad breaks the silence with fake throat-clearing noises, the sounds he makes when he wants attention, not when he's choking on something. He's looking at me, and his eyebrows are raised and his eyes are big like he's enjoying a joke. "Sounds like your mom's taken a new psychology course, eh Munchkin?"

"I. Have. Not," says Mom.

Trouble on the horizon. Surely Dad can tell?

But Dad ignores her and continues to talk to me as if Mom isn't even there. "Because as we both know, the minute your mom picks up a new psychological theory, she makes communication in the English language as intelligible as Martian."

He's right, and part of me wants to laugh, but I take a peek at Mom and a bigger part of me decides laughing wouldn't be a good idea.

"Really?" says Mom. "Well, if you want to keep looking at life through the same old lens using the same old ideas, be my guest. I'm not going to apologize for learning something new and trying to share it with my family." She half turns to me, as though she's still expecting me to come up with an answer.

"You can't expect Sylvie to answer a question like that," says Dad. "I couldn't answer it myself. What's wrong with an old-fashioned question like, *How was your day?*"

"That is not a good quality question," says Mom. "Family time should include good quality conversation, and that requires good quality questions. Most people don't answer those *How-was-your-day?* questions very well. Their days are a lot of things, so they answer with something inane, like *fine*."

Dad raises one eyebrow and looks in my direction. He's hoping I'm going to say something sassy, but even though I'll disappoint him by not joining in on his fun, I'm not going to do it, not this time. I give him a little confused smile, and hope that Mom doesn't take it the wrong way.

"I could show you an excellent journal article on the subject," says Mom.

"That explains it," says Dad, throwing up his hands.

Mom points her fork at him. "Do you mean to tell me that if I asked you if there were any times today that you felt proud of yourself, you wouldn't be able to answer?"

"I'm always proud of myself," says Dad, straightening in his chair and puffing out his chest. He cocks his head to one side. He looks like a cartoon character.

But I can tell Mom doesn't think he's funny.

I want to yell at them to be nice to each other, but Dad would say he was only teasing and why can't anyone take a joke, and Mom would say she was only trying to create a meaningful family experience. I stare at my plateful of unappealing food. It looked good enough five minutes ago, but now I couldn't swallow a thing. I feel the same cloud of helplessness I experienced earlier this afternoon when Kansas was telling me about her difficulties. And somehow it dawns on me: I realize I did do something to feel proud of today. So before Mom can retaliate, I say, "I had a good conversation with Kansas today, and I listened to her and tried to be supportive, and it was really difficult because I didn't know what to say."

Mom nods her approval, which means I've sided with her and not Dad, and that wasn't my intention. I have to balance things out, and in a mental tumble realize this would be a good time to engage Dad with some questions he likes to answer. "Dad, maybe you can help here. Kansas is having financial problems. Well, not right now, but she's looking into the future—" (Dad will like this, he says most people don't plan their finances far enough ahead) "—and thinks she might have to sell Hambone to cover expenses."

"Horses are expensive, and so is having a family," says Dad.

"Was I expensive?"

"You were worth every penny," says Dad. "You were a bargain."

This is extremely high praise coming from my dad. Bargains are everything to him.

"Now isn't this a good quality conversation?" says Mom.

"It sure is!" I say. Even though it is and it isn't. I have helped to avert a family table-top war, I had a compliment from my dad, but I'm no closer to finding a solution for Kansas. "Kansas says this baby is going to be more expensive than most."

"I wonder what she means by that?" says Mom, which is a surprise—I thought she would know.

"Maybe she's having twins," says Dad. "That would be twice as expensive."

"I think she'd have told me if there were twins," I say.

"Well, you never know," says Dad.

Mom has fallen strangely silent. I catch her staring at

me, then she pokes at her dinner with her fork, and I can tell there's something seriously wrong even before she asks, "How was school today, Honey?"

I want to say *fine*, because the less I say about school today, the better. But obviously I can't say *fine*, not after Mom's recent lecture. I'm struggling with what I might say when I'm literally saved by the bell—the front door bell. The door whooshes open and in waltzes Auntie Sally.

"Anybody home?" she yodels from the entranceway. "Am I in time for a glass of wine?"

"Our lucky night," mutters Dad.

"In here, Sally," calls Mom.

My saviour, Auntie Sally, arrives in the dining room like a human kissing machine. She smooches each of us on the cheek before collapsing into the fourth chair at the table. My cousin Erika slides into the room behind her. Erika is Taylor's younger sister. She's only eleven, but she's eight inches taller than me and thinks that qualifies her to treat me like a baby, if she bothers to acknowledge me at all. She flops into the extra chair in the corner, well away from the table, pulls out her iPod and thumbs away.

Auntie Sally says, "You won't believe the day I've had." She points a finger at me. "Never work in retail, Sylvie. It'll kill you. Get a good education and have a profession like your mother. You're lucky you can't ever have babies, they totally destroy your career path... sorry, Erika, but it's true."

Sorry, Erika? What about *Sorry, Sylvia*? I'm *lucky I can't have babies*? I know people with Turners usually can't conceive, but does she have to talk about it like this? I don't know what to say.

Dad says, "Well, it's great to see you, Sally. Sorry, I have to go mow the lawn." He leaves the table. He mowed the lawn on Saturday. If I behaved like that, my parents would say I'm rude and inhospitable.

"If I'd stuck with my first job, I'd be a CEO by now," continues Auntie Sally, then launches into her employment history from around the beginning of time.

Mom smiles vacantly and her eyes flick to Erika. Mom has told me she thinks Erika has an Internet addiction. I can see the wheels turning as she decides how to bring this up if Auntie Sally pauses long enough to permit a change of topic.

Auntie Sally's monologue shifts seamlessly to a description of her early dating years, before she married the first time. I edge my chair away from the table. I didn't think she'd catch the motion, but she does. "What about you, Sylvie, are you dating yet? Oh, I suppose not, you haven't started using those estrogen patches have you?"

The shock takes my breath away. My mom has been blabbing to Auntie Sally about my personal private life. Everyone in town will know.

I stare at my mom. She drops her eyes to her placemat. Good—she feels guilty, and she should.

"Erika has her first boyfriend," says Auntie Sally, not noticing a thing.

"Here she goes," says Erika without looking up from her screen. Obviously, she's more used to being made a public spectacle than I am.

Auntie Sally says, "He's a much nicer boy than the ones Taylor tends to rescue out of the gutter, that's for sure. I don't know where she got that tendency but if Sylvie develops—"

Mom says, "Sylvie, would you mind popping out to the grocery store for me and buying a carton of orange juice for breakfast? You can take the cash out of my purse."

I don't speak. I push back my chair and flee the room. Auntie Sally carries on, as does Erika, and my mom is left to deal with them on her own, as she deserves.

Chapter Nine

I take a twenty-dollar bill out of Mom's wallet. If there had been a fifty, I would have taken that instead.

I wish people didn't talk as much as they do. The facts can be difficult enough to bear, but they're ten times more impossible after people put words to them and say them out loud.

I've known I probably can't have kids of my own ever since I was diagnosed with Turners almost a year ago. I always figured that given a choice, I'd want puppies and kittens and ponies instead of a baby. But when I realized I didn't have a choice, that becoming pregnant was likely never going to be an option, I admit I felt sad. Sometimes I still feel a little sad. But hearing Auntie Sally go on about it as though it was nothing made me mad. How is it possible for a grown woman to be such a bonehead?

Of course, I can always adopt, that's what Mom says. Well, fine. Maybe some day when I grow up if I can't have a horse, I'll adopt a baby.

I buy the orange juice and treat myself to a dark chocolate bar for dessert. Mom doesn't approve of me eating chocolate after dinner because she thinks the caffeine will ruin my sleep. I think I could have an awesome jet-fuelled lucid dream with the help of caffeine. I could ride a cross-country with Olympic-sized jumps.

I try to buy scratch-and-win lottery tickets with the remaining money, but the cashier says she's not allowed to sell tickets to minors. Instead I buy a bag of organic carrots for Brooklyn, a pack of gum for emergencies like finding Topaz crying in the hallway, and two more chocolate bars for me. There's twenty cents left over.

I'm having a good chomp, walking down the street, still a couple of blocks from home, and I'm really enjoying myself— thinking about life and dreams, eating chocolate—and decide to extend my stroll with a loop along the oceanside trail. There's a shortcut to the trail if I sneak through the gated retirement community, which I've done in the past, reluctantly, with Taylor who isn't concerned about breaking trespass laws. Generally, I'd rather go the long way even if it means an extra ten minutes. Tonight I'm feeling more a badass.

As I round the bend in the road I see that the gate to the retirement community is wide open and there are Open House signs pointing up the driveway. Surely, I can't be arrested for trespassing if there's an Open House. I hesitate for a moment at the road's edge, but then feel a rush of I don't know what, maybe it's the caffeine, and I walk in like I own the place. If anyone stops me I'll say I'm someone's grandchild. And besides, there's my new mantra: I have faced danger before.

I swing the grocery bag, enjoying the excitement of breaking a law, feeling good about myself. Cowgirl tough. I can be like that too. An old guy totters stiffly out of the condo with the Open House sign. Even if he wanted to arrest me he'd never be able to catch me. His shoulders are round and his legs are bowed. I hope I don't look like that when I'm old—it must be awful to not be able to run and skip, and to have to worry about falling all the time. The man checks the display on his cell phone, then slips the phone into a hip pocket. He looks kind of like my grandpa, but my grandpa refuses to buy a cell phone no matter how much my mom begs him, plus he lives in Saskatchewan, so I know it's not really him, though it feels nice to be reminded of him. And I am *really* reminded, because the closer I get, the more the guy looks like Grandpa. And then a lady comes out the front door and takes his arm, and she looks *exactly* like Grandpa's girlfriend Isobel, and I'm thinking, *what the heck is going on here?* Not just because they would never be in town without telling us, but also because last time I saw them they didn't look this old. They can't have changed that much in a few months. Could it be that, whenever I'm with them, they're just Grandpa and Isobel, and only when I see them unexpectedly do I notice that they are worn-out old people? It's shocking. How could I have been so blind?

Then they see me.

They stop dead in their tracks. Though maybe I shouldn't say *dead*.

"Grandpa? Isobel?" I say. "Why aren't you in Saskatchewan?"

"Hey, Pipsqueak," says Grandpa. "You caught us. We're house-hunting."

"We didn't want anyone to know," says Isobel. "Not until we'd made up our minds. We didn't want you to be disappointed if it didn't work out."

"Hardly that," says Grandpa. "We didn't want the pressure. Or the interference. Our kids treat us like nincompoops."

Isobel jabs him with her elbow.

"You're moving here?" I am bouncing on my toes with happiness.

"There's a good chance," says Grandpa. He gestures to the unit behind them. "That's a pretty nice place. We have to work out the financing though."

"My dad could... "

I stop because Grandpa is shaking his head. "Sorry, Sylvia. Not a word to anyone—not to your parents, or to your Auntie Sally. They'll all have their opinions on what's best for us, and they won't agree with each other, and it'll turn into a complete kerfuffle. Isobel and I are going to bumble along as best we can, using our years and years of experience, and then live with the consequences of our decision. Right Isobel?"

Isobel nods. "That's right, Henry. Though I'm not at all happy with putting Sylvia in the position of keeping a secret from her parents."

Grandpa sighs. "Evelyn does have her rules forbidding family secrets... "

"You can trust me," I say. I would love to be trusted with a secret. This will be so much better than being excluded, like I am on that expensive baby issue no one wants to discuss with me. "And it's not really a secret. It's more a surprise, don't you think?"

Chapter Ten

Auntie Sally and Erika have left by the time I get home. I stash the carrots, gum and chocolate bars in the garage near my bike.

Mom is hanging up the phone when I come in the door with the orange juice. I tuck the carton in the refrigerator then stuff the plastic bag and empty chocolate bar wrapper deep in the garbage container under the sink.

"You were quick," says Mom.

"I was?"

"I'm just off the phone from trying to call your Grandpa."

My heart lurches in my chest. My secret-keeping abilities are being put to the test much sooner than I expected. "Was his line busy?" A clever diversion, if I do say so myself.

"There was no answer," she says. "I didn't think too much of it when I tried earlier, but then Sally said she hasn't been able to reach him either, and he's not returning messages. I hope he's okay."

"I'm sure he's fine, Mom," I say. I struggle for the right tone so I don't sound too completely sure of myself, even though I am, due to the fact that he looked perfectly fine ten minutes ago when I left him at the retirement village.

But she doesn't pay any attention to me or my tone. "It's so unlike him. I wish he wasn't so stubborn about not buying a cell phone. I've tried and tried to talk him into it, but he keeps saying they're too expensive and he's too old to learn new technology."

I barely manage to stop myself from mentioning that there may be some change on this front.

"Maybe I should phone his girlfriend Isobel," Mom continues, "but I'm ashamed to admit that I don't know her last name. Do you know her last name?" She doesn't wait for me to answer. "Sally may know." She grabs the phone and hits the speed dial for Auntie Sally. She taps her front tooth rapidly with a fingernail. I wonder how far I can let this surprise run if it means my mom is going to have a nervous breakdown, because obviously even if Auntie Sally has Isobel's number or knows her last name, Isobel isn't going to be picking up her phone either.

But Auntie Sally doesn't answer, and Mom hangs up without leaving a message. "I talked to him last weekend and everything sounded fine, and he didn't tell me he was going away. Maybe he's fallen and can't get up."

"Mom. You're letting worry take over. Stop." This is the sort of thing she says to me when I am anxious. "Remember to visualize a red Stop sign."

She looks at me and focuses briefly. "You're right, Pumpkin, I have to externalize the problem." She draws a deep breath and puffs it out. She's trying to blow worry right out of the room; I know, she's told me to do it a hundred thousand times. "It's not so easy when it's for yourself," says Mom after the third big puff. "I just wish he had a cell phone, or a medic alert system, or something."

"Mom, I know that Grandpa's old, but he has years and years of experience," I say.

The quotation stops her in her tracks. "That's wise of you, Sylvie. You're right. I just worry. Wait until I'm your elderly parent, and then you'll know what it's like."

I try to picture my mom as an elderly parent, wobbling on a cane, still trying to run my life. "Right," I say.

"I guess I want him to live forever, without suffering. Silly me." She pulls a shredded tissue from her pocket and blows her nose. "Why does he have to be in Saskatchewan? It's so far away, and in the middle of nowhere."

"Maybe we should ask him to move here!" I make my eyes big as if this amazing thought has only occurred to me this very second. I am an Ace Conspirator.

Mom's eyes get big too. "Oh, no, Honey, that would not be a good idea."

She reads the disappointment on my face.

"I mean it would be good if he moved closer, of course. A nearby city like Victoria would be nice. But not here, no I don't think so. I need a little more space than that. And so does your father."

"I don't mean he should move into our house!" I say. Is that what she thought I meant? "Wouldn't it be nice to have him in town though? Or in the neighbourhood? We could see him all the time instead of just on vacations."

Mom frowns. "I wouldn't want him to become dependent on us. We wouldn't want his social circle to shrink to the size of our family—it wouldn't be healthy for him. He has friends in Saskatchewan, and they're important."

"Mom, his friends are all dead, except for Isobel. What if Isobel moved out too?"

Mom flaps her hands as if to erase the whole notion from the air. "No, no. Now you're in fantasy land, Pumpkin."

"Isobel has a son here in town, that's how she and Grandpa met. They were both flying here to visit with family, and had adjoining seats on the plane—remember?"

There's a moment of silence while Mom considers this with (from the look on her face) increasing horror. I hear the front door open and close, and Dad appears in the kitchen.

"Has your sister gone home?" he asks Mom.

Mom blinks at him.

"What's going on?" he says.

I leave it to Mom to explain, hoping she will address my confusion too. Why wouldn't she want Grandpa living closer? And should I break it to her that it's not fantasy at all, but a wonderful surprising fact?

"Sally and I have been trying to reach my dad for a few days now," says Mom. "He hasn't answered the phone or returned any messages. I was getting a little concerned. So Pumpkin here was suggesting that it might be easier if Grandpa lived closer to us instead of halfway across the world in Saskatchewan."

Dad snorts. "It's only a few hundred kilometres away. Hardly *halfway around the world.*"

This is so not true. I've checked on Google maps and it's more like 2,000 kilometres.

Mom shrugs. "Well that's really not the point, is it? I'd be concerned about him losing his independence if he moved closer to us. We don't want to be living in each others' pockets."

I study Dad carefully. In the past he hasn't always appreciated Grandpa the way I do or Mom does. Dad never said he was grateful that Grandpa bought Brooklyn for me, and I think there are bigger issues. Once Dad referred to Grandpa as an *interfering old goat.* I don't expect him to be terribly concerned for Grandpa's sense of independence.

Dad draws breath for what I can tell will be a fiery response but he looks at me and catches himself. He clears his throat and turns back to Mom. "He's probably on a bingo bus trip and forgot to tell you about it. If there was something wrong, you'd have heard."

Mom isn't listening. "Maybe I should call his local RCMP detachment and ask them to look in on him. Unless you can remember Isobel's last name?"

She wants to call the police? This is terrible, but if I confess that I bumped into Grandpa and Isobel less than an hour ago and three blocks away, will I start a more epic catastrophe?

Dad walks over and takes Mom in a big hug. "Whatever makes you feel better, Ev," he says. "I think you're over-reacting, I think he's probably fine, but if it helps you worry less, you go right ahead." I'm thinking *Wow, Dad!* And then he ruins it by adding, "I'm sure the police would welcome a change from chasing criminals and investigating highway crashes or whatever else they have do in Saskatchewan."

Mom stiffens and pushes him away, and before I am forced to ruin Grandpa's surprise, she bolts from the kitchen, Dad in pursuit saying, "I was kidding. Where's your sense of humour?"

Their bedroom door slams (Mom) then opens and closes more appropriately (Dad) and then all I hear is intense muffled voices.

Maybe I should have said something.

Chapter Eleven

In the morning, there are two fresh emails from Taylor. One links to *DiscoverFairHorsemanship.com*. The other, strangely, appears to have nothing to do with horses: *The Chakras and Spiritual Growth*. Now what is she getting at? I'm almost tempted to read it. But I don't. Reason prevails. Delete delete.

Dad has left for work already, and Mom is heading out early for her Pilates class when I arrive in the kitchen.

"We still haven't discussed those safety issues with regard to eventing," she says before leaving. "Don't think I've forgotten, because I haven't."

Great. I eat my Shreddies alone. In peace.

Logan Losino is waiting for me inside the door of math class. He shuffles me into the corner behind the door. Mr. Brumby will be arriving any second now, so he'll have to make this quick.

"Where've you been, Sylvia? I've been looking for you," he says.

"I was looking for you, too," I say, because I was, for a short while, before I found out that he thinks I'm handicapped. Still, it's a bit of a stretch, so I can't look him in the eye.

"Are you okay? Has something happened?"

"Topaz and I were sent to the office for fighting." I've thrown him a bone. This is ancient history, and I don't even care about it any more.

A patch of red appears on his neck. "Topaz hit you?"

"I kicked her. Mr. Brumby saw it. She called me a freak."

Logan puts his hand on my arm. Through my sleeve, I can feel his palm is warm and damp, and I like it despite myself.

"You're not a freak, Sylvia."

He's being so nice. Logan is always nice to me. But what if he's only nice because he feels sorry for me because he thinks I'm handicapped? I couldn't endure it. I slide past him. "I have to take my seat. Mr. Brumby's going to be watching me closely for a while. I can't give him any excuses. I need to be careful—he can be very unprofessional."

I slither past Topaz, who is already sitting down. Her fingers are stuck in her hair, twirling. I glimpse the bald patch, which is bigger than it was yesterday.

Logan takes his seat behind mine. He leans forward and whispers in my ear just as Mr. Brumby strides in the door. "Can I see you in the cafeteria at lunch?"

Mr. Brumby glares at Logan. "Time for math class, not socializing," he says, saving me from having to answer. I don't know if I want to meet Logan or not.

Of course, class proceeds to be a disaster. It's always an ordeal for me: try as I might the concepts will not stick in my brain. What is a number anyway? Mr. Brumby makes it obvious that he is keeping an eye on both me and Topaz. He actually singles me out for a question even though he knows how much I struggle with math. Of course, I get the answer completely wrong, and Topaz laughs, so then he asks her a question and she gets it wrong too. But I don't laugh because I notice she's pulling more hairs out of her head. I pull a hair out of my own scalp to see what it feels like, and it hurts and sure isn't anything I'd want to do repeatedly. There must be something seriously wrong with her. She didn't sound happy when I found her in the hallway yesterday, and it must be beyond agonizing to live with her twin Amber. I realize I feel sorry for her, and it doesn't seem to be a terrible way to feel about someone, though I still don't want anyone feeling sorry for me, especially if it's Logan Losino. And then, because it's math class and I have never been able to concentrate on things I don't understand, I start wondering what's going on with Kansas's baby, and what's wrong with my mom and dad, why are they always on each others' cases instead of supporting each other the way that Grandpa and Isobel do? And did I do the right thing by not telling my parents that I'd seen Grandpa and Isobel? Is having a surprise worth all this trouble? Though, it's not just the surprise that would be ruined if I told—Grandpa would be upset about my parents meddling in his affairs. And Mom and Dad would be upset about Grandpa losing his independence by moving too close to us. None of which makes any sense to me.

I'm deep in thought, contemplating all these life difficulties, when I realize Mr. Brumby is looking at me expectantly. He must have asked me another question. Two in one class. And I'm totally lost. I have no idea what he's been talking about or what he asked me. In my peripheral vision, I can see Logan's hand shoot up as he volunteers to provide the right answer and draw Mr. Brumby's attention, but Mr. Brumby isn't falling for it this time. Logan stabs the air repeatedly, muttering, "I got it. I know this one." I know he's not showing off, I know he's doing this for me, he's done it before, but Mr. Brumby ignores him.

"Sylvia," he says. I can see the frustration on his face. Should I remind him about anger and danger? Probably not. I hope he doesn't mock me. I hope he doesn't shout or make ironic comments or call me Pipsqueak in front of the whole class. I feel hot and sweaty and my heart is pounding fast, just like I felt when Brooklyn and I finished the cross-country course after almost falling and dying at the last fence. Well, I survived that. I sit up straight in my chair. Mr. Brumby draws a deep breath. "Pay attention," he says.

Pay attention? That's it?

Logan lowers his hand to his desk with a thump. Even he can't believe it. "Is Mr. Brumby smoking weed?" he murmurs.

Mr. Brumby is still looking at me as though he expects a response.

"I'll pay attention now," I say. And for some reason I add, "Thank you." And Mr. Brumby smiles at me. It's not a real smile. It's brief and stiff and fake, like a muscle spasm, or like something he's practiced in front of the mirror, though not quite often enough. I have no idea what's come over him.

Chapter Twelve

I hide in the library at lunch. I eat my sandwich there, which is strictly against the rules. I have to be really careful with the plastic wrap to make sure it makes no noise, and I eat with teeny little mouse nibbles, so instead of chewing normal mouthfuls I basically suck my sandwich to death, which is not easy because, of course, it's made with nutritious whole grain bread and some parts of that do not want to dissolve.

I can't face Logan right now. I'm too confused. I like that he tries to protect me from Amber and Mr. Brumby, and I like that he listens to me. Sometimes he gets a soppy expression on his face when he sees me that reminds me of how I might look if I'd found an abandoned puppy. Maybe he does this because he feels sorry for me, or maybe he feels something else, but I have no clue what he's thinking. I suppose I should feel great about how important I am to Logan for whatever reason, and maybe I would if I felt the same, but I don't. I like him, but not the way he seems to like me. The imbalance leaves me uncomfortable, and I have no idea how to fix it. I don't want Logan to feel less, but I can't seem to feel more. I don't know if there's something lacking about the relationship, or something lacking in me.

I avoid Logan after school too, and make my way to the barn. I want to wrap my arms around Brooklyn's neck and tell him all my troubles and listen to him breathe and smell his grassy breath, and then I'll be fine.

Except that Kansas intercepts me as I'm leaning my bike against the barn wall. "Come to the house for a cup of tea," she says.

Tea and a lecture. No, thank you. "But I need to ride Brooklyn. I have to keep him in shape for our next cross-country competition."

"You're right, but this is important. It won't take long. You can ride afterwards. Declan and I need to talk to you."

This sounds ominous. Are they splitting? Have they found a buyer for Hambone? Do they want to sign me up for babysitting? Of all the awful things, that seems most likely, and the worst, because I do not like taking care of babies. Taylor would be a much better choice, she is older and more mature and has on-the-job experience.

I have no opportunity to point this out because Kansas has left me and is lumbering towards her little house. I trot after her and catch up at the top of the steps. She is holding the door open for me.

I haven't been inside for a couple of weeks and it's changed a lot. Before it felt like a hollow construction site, and now it's a home. It's a tiny home, but there is way more room than Kansas had in the travel trailer. It probably seems more spacious than it really is because they still don't have much in the way of furniture. There's a little wooden table and three plastic chairs like we have on our patio. There's a tray in the middle of the table, and on it is Kansas's teapot with the tea cozy her mom knitted for her, three mugs and a milk and sugar container, none of them matching. There's an open package of digestive cookies. Declan is eating one as I come in the door. He swallows it quickly, then pulls out a chair for me. He doesn't usually act like such a gentleman. I wish he'd treat me normally, as this is making me feel very uneasy. They must desperately want me for babysitting. I'll be sorry to disappoint them, but I'm not going to do it. I don't care how short of money they are—it won't be a good idea.

Their German shepherd dog, Bernadette, is lying on her blanket in a corner of the living room. She thumps her tail and looks like she's preparing to get up and come over to see me, but Kansas points one finger at her and tells her to stay. Bernadette's ears fall back with disappointment, and she drops her head between her paws, and wags the end of her tail hopefully. Kansas can be quite strict. She has that side to her. I hope she doesn't use it to make me babysit. I'd rather clean stalls. I'd rather tidy the manure pile or pick paddocks or scrub out water buckets or any one of a zillion tasks to do with the horses.

Kansas sits at the table with me and pours us each a mug of tea. She adds milk exactly the way I like it, and puts three heaping spoonfuls of sugar in Declan's mug, which is quite shocking because my mom says sugar is poison and from what I've read about nutrition, I'd have to agree with her. Declan takes his seat beside Kansas and holds her hand. He is so romantic. Or maybe he's just grateful for all the sugar.

Kansas drums the fingers of her free hand on the arm of her chair. "Sylvia, there's something we need to discuss with you. Declan wondered if we needed your parents' permission, but in the end, we decided you're mature enough to hear it directly from us first."

I take a sip of tea and reach for a cookie. I am not going to be flattered into babysitting.

"It's about the baby," says Kansas.

I nod. Here it comes. Kansas is going to need lots of help because Declan will be working extra hours and can I please learn to change stinking diapers. No, no, no. I dunk my cookie in my tea.

And then my world changes.

"Something showed up on the ultrasound, so we had a prenatal genetic screening test," says Kansas.

My cookie falls apart and drifts out of sight to the bottom of the mug. My heart is pounding like crazy. There's something wrong with the baby? That's what I'm thinking in my head, but it's too terrible a question to ask out loud.

"We found out a while ago. We had a lot to think about, and then we weren't sure how to tell you."

"How to tell me?" I have found my voice. What has this got to do with me? I'm staring at Kansas, but something's hit her mute button.

"They think the baby may have Turner Syndrome," says Declan.

"No way," I say.

"Yeah, like what are the chances of that?" says Kansas with a fake laugh. "It's such a rare condition, and then to know two people... "

"We thought you should know," says Declan. "Before anyone else."

"I know we left it late to tell you," says Kansas. "I kept putting it off while we sorted out our options. The genetic counsellor had offered us amniocentesis so we'd know for sure, but there were risks to that."

"More for mares than for humans," says Declan.

"Declan, I know," says Kansas with a note of exasperation.

"But I'd read all the studies about mares miscarrying after amnio. I'd never forgive myself." From her tone, I guess they've had this conversation many times before.

"And she is a boss mare," I remind Declan.

"She is that," he says with a small smile.

"We didn't want you to worry," says Kansas.

Worry? I'm going to know someone else with Turners! It's all I can do to contain my joy. I wrap my ankles around the chair legs to stop my feet from dancing.

"I don't know if this is appropriate," I say, "because, of course, all I want for you is to have a baby with the least complications possible... but I feel like I'm finally going to have a sister."

Declan and Kansas both laugh—a real laugh, full of warmth.

"That's kind of how we felt at the beginning too," says Kansas. "But then the doctors started telling us more about the syndrome and how it's different for everyone who has it. Some people are quite handicapped—" She stops abruptly and Declan clasps his free hand over top of their already holding hands.

"And other people are unstoppable fantastic individuals, such as yourself," says Declan.

"This is why the baby may be expensive?" I say. "Because she may need hearing aids, or heart surgery?" Heart surgery. For a baby. What could be worse than that for new parents?

"Fortunately, her heart seems okay," says Kansas. "We had a prenatal cardiac ultrasound. But at some point, she'll need human growth hormone, which is wicked expensive and may not be covered by health insurance."

I know about growth hormone, having been on it for a while until I had an ultra-rare side effect, but I had no idea it was expensive or who paid for it. Did my parents have to come up with extra money for that?

"And then she'll need help with her learning disabilities," says Kansas.

"Learning disabilities? Not necessarily!" I say.

Kansas and Declan exchange a look then Kansas shrugs. "Well, maybe not. But that's what the doctors say."

"But I don't have learning disabilities!" I insist.

"The particulars don't really matter," says Declan, though I'm not so sure about that, and I'm about to make my point even more clearly when Kansas interrupts.

"We haven't told anyone else, except for my mother," says Kansas. "We thought you should be the first to know."

I nod. This makes sense. Of course they would want me to know. And they would want to consult with me. For the first time in my life, I am actually the expert on something. It's beyond awesome. Kansas and Declan are so cool and wonderful, and I am lucky to have them as friends.

"There's a babysitting course offered through the recreation centre," I tell them. "I can sign up next week. Taylor took it already, and she babysits all the time, but she doesn't know much about Turner Syndrome. I'll be good at that."

Yes, I will.

After tea, I tack up Brooklyn and take him for a hack around the fields. We warm up at the walk even though he doesn't want to—he breaks pace to trot repeatedly, and tosses his head each time I insist that he do as I ask. I make him walk and make him walk, because Kansas is always telling me that I'm the one in charge and Brooklyn can't be allowed to set the agenda, but eventually, I think what the heck, let's go, and he pops into a big swingy trot. His head is up; his back is loose. This is what I like best about riding: I'm up there going with the flow.

The back corner of the field is out of view of the house,

and that's where I say, "Brooklyn, you can canter if you want." That's all I need to do. I don't touch him with my leg; he is so smart he understands complete sentences. We loop around the back of the field, and from there, I can see Kansas watching from the doorway of her house, so I take the reins in one hand and wave with the other. She gives me a cautious little wave back. I can tell what she's thinking, it's like Morse code for *Do not gallop your horse, Sylvia.* I pick up my reins and ask Brooklyn to trot, which he does eventually, but then when we circle back to the place where Kansas can't see us I tell him he can do whatever he wants. I feel his hind-quarters come under, and in no time at all, we are galloping flat-out along the fence line, the tears streaming from the wind in my face, and I ride and ride like the unstoppable fantastic person I am.

Chapter Thirteen

I have to walk Brooklyn around the field for about half an hour to cool him out before returning to the barn. If Kansas found him later, all sweaty in his stall, she'd know what we were up to, and obviously, she has enough to worry about right now without adding me and Brooklyn to her list. And to be honest, I have enough to worry about myself without having to deal with Kansas's anxiety.

This means I'm a bit late when I get back to the barn, and I'm going to have to be speedy to make it home in time for dinner.

There's a strange car in the parking lot with a National Car Rentals sticker on the bumper, but no people in sight.

I dismount at the barn door and lead Brooklyn down the alleyway toward his stall. Hambone stretches over his half-door like he always does and tries to bite Brooklyn's bum. Brooklyn sees this coming like he always does and steps to the side at precisely the right moment, taking the least possible effort and with no change in expression, as though this game has grown stale. I'm thinking how fortunate I am to have such an unflappable horse, when Brooklyn leaps sideways and almost stomps my foot.

"What the heck's got into you?" I ask. I follow his gaze to the tack room door. Is someone hiding in there? An axe murderer? A crazy animal rights person from PETA who is going to set all the horses free from their paddock-prisons so they can be mushed by a transport truck on the highway? I drag Brooklyn closer until I can kick the door open with my boot. And there's Grandpa and Isobel trying to hide under a horse blanket.

"Grandpa?" I say. "What are you doing in there? You frightened Brooklyn." Not me, of course.

"Sorry to scare you, Brooklyn," he says, walking over and patting him on the face. Brooklyn turns his head away—he hates being patted on the forehead. I usually tell people this, but don't want to hurt Grandpa's feelings. "You're not expecting your parents to show up here today, are you Pipsqueak?" says Grandpa. "Because Isobel and I are flying back to Saskatchewan tonight and we wanted to check in with you first on how the surprise is going."

"You're safe here, Grandpa. And I haven't told anyone about your big plans."

"Not even Dakota? I thought you would have told her."

"You mean Kansas," I tell him for the millionth time. It must be awful to be old. "And no, I haven't told her either."

He looks really happy about that, though Isobel seems less enthused. She has finished refolding the horse blanket and is trying to brush dust and horse hair off her slacks.

"We've put in an offer, so there's nothing to do now but wait," he says. "Do you think you can keep it under your hat for a while longer?"

"No problem," I say. "But you might want to give Mom

a call. She's been phoning your house for days and not getting an answer. She's thinking about calling the police to check to make sure you haven't had a fall."

Isobel says, "Oh Henry, did you forget to call Evelyn?"

Grandpa says, "I'm not accounting to my children for every move I make. Especially now. It would set a bad precedent."

Isobel takes his hand. "But Evelyn's been worried, Henry."

"For no reason," says Grandpa. "She's always worried about something."

"And I'm sure it's putting Sylvia in a very difficult position," says Isobel softly.

I'm glad Isobel mentioned that so I don't have to. Isobel always knows just the right thing to say.

"Right," says Grandpa. "Okay, I concede the point. I'll call her as soon as we get home."

"You could call now, on your cell," says Isobel.

"Not on your life," says Grandpa. "I'm sure Evelyn has caller ID and there's no way she's learning that I have my own cell phone. She'll be checking up on me all the time, I won't have a moment's privacy for the rest of my life."

"We could use a pay phone at the airport," says Isobel. "Would that work, Sylvia?"

I'm always impressed with how smart Isobel is, and on top of that I am extremely appreciative that she has included me in the planning. She never treats me like a kid. Maybe she and Grandpa will marry after they leave Saskatchewan. Maybe there are rules in the seniors village about this, so people have to be married and not live common-law, like Kansas and Declan. They would ask me to be in the wedding party. I'd like that, except Mom would want me to wear a dress, and I'd refuse, and it would be a big mess. Isobel is watching me. I've gotten ahead of myself.

"I guess you could phone from the airport. I don't know

how pay phones show on call display," I say. I don't know much about being sneaky. Other than galloping behind the trees.

"Henry, you can tell her the same thing I told my son," says Isobel. "We found a last-minute deal on a trip to Reno and jumped at the chance."

Grandpa nods. "A week of gambling, eating, drinking and dancing girls. Evelyn will believe that all right, especially if we have airport noises in the background. And it'll give her a whole new parcel of things to worry about."

Sometimes I think my grandpa isn't very mature.

Chapter Fourteen

Dad and I have just taken our seats at the dinner table when the phone rings. Mom is carrying her plate from the kitchen. We were all late coming home so it's scrambled eggs with cheese on toast, which I love and Mom only makes when she's desperate for time. She hasn't had a chance to ask us a good quality question or to pressure me to give up riding, and I haven't been able to let them know that Kansas's baby is going to have Turner Syndrome.

The phone rings again. Usually we don't pick up phone calls that come in during meal times, but I figure this could be Grandpa calling from the airport so I'm halfway off my chair when my mom tells me to stay put, pointing a finger at me the same way Kansas issued a command to her dog. How demeaning. Mom checks the call display on her way by, "Unavailable," she reads. "Must be telemarketers. They always phone at dinner time. They have no respect for families." She leaves it for the answering machine and takes her seat, but as soon as she hears Grandpa's voice over the speaker she vaults from the table, toppling her chair over backwards, and grabs the phone.

"Dad! Where are you? I've been worried about you, um, a little. I mean, I know you're okay, but you weren't answering and didn't return my messages—"

My dad rolls his eyes. "A little worried," he says. "Right."

"You went to Reno?" asks Mom.

"He better not have gambled away all his pension money," says Dad.

"With Isobel?" says Mom. "Well, that's nice. That's really nice." Her voice is starting to sound more normal. "You know, I thought about calling Isobel when I couldn't reach you... No, of course I wouldn't phone the police."

Well, isn't that the biggest, fattest lie I've heard all day? Dad and I have an almost invisible laugh together.

Mom says, "But the funny thing is, no one knew her last name, so I couldn't look up her number."

I'm back to eating my dinner, relaxing because I don't have to manage a secret for the moment. Everything can work out over time. In the end, there will be a great surprise for Mom and Dad, and I'll have lots of fun visiting Grandpa and Isobel when they live closer, and life is pretty good sometimes, and that's when my mom says, "Brumby? That name sounds familiar. Maybe you did tell us before."

I put down my fork. I may never eat again. How many Brumbys can there be? Isobel's last name is Brumby? That would mean she'd have to be Mr. Brumby's mother. Oh no. If Grandpa marries Isobel, I'm going to be related to Mr. Brumby. What could be worse than that?

Mom is so relieved when she finishes the call that she fills a glass of wine from the carton in the refrigerator and takes a big glug before she sits back down. "All that worrying for nothing," she says.

"I'm not saying a word," says Dad. "My lips are sealed." Then he goes to the kitchen and pours a glass of wine for himself. This is so unfair. If anyone needs a drink right now, it's me.

"Brumby," says Mom thoughtfully. "Isn't that—"

"Sylvie's fascist math teacher?" says Dad.

"Tony," says Mom, "he's not a fascist."

Dad swallows some wine. "You're the one who said he had poor teaching skills, Ev."

"I wouldn't criticize one of Sylvie's teachers," says Mom.

"You said he knew nothing about motivation," I remind her. "You said he lacked a basic understanding of psychology and human nature. You said he had anger management issues."

"That doesn't make him a fascist," says Mom. "He must be Isobel's son. He can't be too bad; she's a fairly nice person."

Fairly nice? Isobel is awesome. Mr. Brumby was probably adopted, late in life.

"Though, I have to say," says Mom, "that Isobel might not be the best influence on Grandpa—up to now he's always been very good about keeping us informed as to his whereabouts."

I know this is untrue. I know Isobel wanted Grandpa to phone us so no one would worry, and then he decided not to, or he forgot. But I can't very well say anything in her defence without blowing the whole story. I stab my fork into the tablecloth.

"Don't do that, Honey," says Mom. "We should have Mr. Brumby over when Grandpa and Isobel are visiting next time. It would be a nice way of helping her feel welcome in our family."

Oh no. That's a terrible idea. I press the prongs of the fork into my neck. Mom reaches over, draws my hand away and keeps on talking. "Didn't Isobel tell us her son was divorced? Maybe he and Auntie Sally would get along well. We could have a big family get-together. "

"Mom, no, please—"

"Maybe in the summer," says Mom. "That's not for months and months, Sweetie. After school is out. Just once, for a special occasion. It's not as though they live next door and we see them all the time. With the way they're gallivanting around, they may not be interested in seeing us at all!"

"It's hard to compete with Reno," says Dad hopefully.

"True enough," says Mom.

And although it is nice that they are agreeing with each other for a change, and I do really appreciate it, they are both so absolutely wrong.

"Maybe I'll phone him tomorrow and set something up," says Mom.

I have to divert her before something more disastrous happens.

"Mom, there's a girl in my class who's pulling out her own hair!"

"Oh dear," says Mom. She puts down her wine and listens with full attention. Mental health issues always grab her.

"She has a bald spot! It is so gross!" I say. I make my eyes bulge with fake horror.

Mom shakes her head. "She has an impulse control disorder. It's called *trichotillomania*. There are effective cognitive-behavioural treatment protocols available. But she must be deeply unhappy "

"Well, her twin sister is a total evil dork," I say.

"There must be more going on than that. You should be kind to her, Pumpkin," says Mom.

"Why?" asks Dad. "I'm going bald and you're not kind to me."

And off they go again.

Chapter Fifteen

That night I have another lucid dream, which isn't unusual because I can have lucid dreams pretty well whenever I want. What is unusual is who appears. Perhaps I've been under too much stress, because I thought I was well past that stage. Why would I want to dream about a unicorn?

"Why wouldn't you want to dream about me?" asks the unicorn.

The sound of his voice rekindles the annoyance I used to experience when I dreamed about him on a regular basis. Ugh. Who needs this? I take charge and transform the unicorn into Brooklyn but the image doesn't hold—it pops like a soap bubble and there's the unicorn again. I've always had difficulty managing unicorn dreams. He's been lame, and hornless, and generally obnoxious. I haven't dreamed about him for months. His horn has re-grown, which should make him less grumpy; though, there is a new bald spot on the crest of his neck where no mane is sprouting, and he's vain enough that this would be troubling to him.

"I must be regressing," I say.

"You have a lot on your plate," says the unicorn. "Your friendships are in ruin, your pal Kansas's pregnancy is not going as planned, and your whole family is about to be seriously disrupted by the big surprise you're in on. Plus, there's that other major issue you're refusing to face."

"You are harsh."

"Not me—it's reality."

That makes me laugh. "Right—a unicorn talking about reality."

"Laugh if you want to," says the unicorn, "but I'm here any time you need me." And he trots away across the field. He's definitely not lame any more. But he's still annoying.

I don't enjoy being left alone in a big field. I call Brooklyn but he doesn't appear, so I wake myself up. I fluff my pillow and pull my quilt tight under my chin. When I can dream about anything I want, why would I dream about that grumpy old unicorn? It is very puzzling to me. But before I can figure it out, I fall asleep again and don't have any more dreams before the morning.

There is only one fresh email from Taylor, directing me to *Yoga and Horses: Horsemanship as a Spiritual Path*. As usual I delete without reading.

Logan Losino is waiting for me at school, leaning against my locker so I can't open it. I don't think this is intentional on his part, the way it was with Amber, but I am still forced to listen to him, against my will.

"I think you've been avoiding me," says Logan.

I can't tell if he's mad or sad or both. I feel squirmy inside but try not to show it. Everything in my brain has swirled into a muddle, and I don't have a clue what to say.

"I know it's difficult for you to talk about some things,"

says Logan. I don't know what he's talking about and feel more confused than ever. "But I really need to know why you're upset with me."

We have five minutes before class starts, and that doesn't give us much time for a talk, let alone a quality conversation. Not that I know what to say—I haven't rehearsed anything and don't have the right words at hand. I don't like being mad at Logan but don't want him to be mad at me either. I wonder if I can put him off again, tell him we can talk at lunch, or on the weekend. But that would mean feeling yucky for longer and longer. Maybe it would be better to know what's going on with him and get it over with, one way or another.

I could just spill.

I could say the first words that come into my head.

I feel like I'm standing at the edge of a cliff.

"Topaz told me that you told her that I was handicapped," I say, stepping off into space.

"I did?" says Logan.

"She said you told her and Amber that was why they should be nice to me."

Logan wiggles inside his t-shirt. "I might have said something like that. I don't know. But if I did, it would be because I thought they might not pick on you so much if they understood."

"But *handicapped*?" I say. "And now Amber says I'm *special needs*. I hate that."

"I'm sorry," says Logan. "But it's hard to describe Turner Syndrome. What's a *syndrome* anyway?"

He has a point there. I've read a lot about Turner Syndrome and sometimes it's referred to as a *disorder* and other times it's called a *condition*, which is obviously my preference because who wants to think of themselves as *disordered*?

Logan uses his thumbnail to scrape at a piece of tape

that's stuck on the front of my locker. "I'm not sure what *handicapped* or *special needs* mean either. My aunt is in a wheelchair because of MS and she's a lawyer. Taylor's missing a toe, you're short, I'm too skinny, my brother Franco has half a brain... none of us is perfect. You know that."

"You're not too skinny," I say.

He smiles at me for the first time since Monday. His eyes are brown like melted chocolates. He gives me that soppy look. Is this amusement or affection or what? I have to turn away.

"Maybe I was worried that you only liked me because you felt sorry for me," I whisper. I don't want anyone else to hear. I'm not even sure I want Logan to hear.

"Sorry for you?" says Logan. "Because you're short? That's funny."

There's a lot more to Turner Syndrome than being short, but I think I've heard the answer I need without explaining any further. I'm preparing to let it all go when Logan's face reverts to a serious expression. "My mom has a saying: *The undeserved curse cannot alight.* She says it's from the Bible. She quotes it any time I tell her I'm upset that someone is saying bad things about me."

I try to make sense of it, but I can't. "So?" I say.

"So if you don't believe you deserve what someone says about you, it shouldn't stick. But if deep down you're worried they might be right, it does stick and it bothers you."

"But I don't think I'm handicapped or special needs!" I say. I'm sure this has never crossed my mind. But my mind is such a jumble. My face heats up; in seconds it will be glowing like a bonfire. Why am I embarrassed? I'm being ridiculous.

"What's going on?" says Logan. "Is something else upsetting you?"

Something else? No—nothing. Or a million things. My brain whirls. My face is so hot I'm surprised my hair hasn't melted. My armpits are drenched. "I don't know," I say. I can't think.

"Is it something to do with Mr. Brumby?"

My breath catches in my chest. How did Logan find out that Mr. Brumby is about to become my uncle and extend his reign of terror to our family gatherings, where he'll huff and puff and make everyone sit quietly and behave themselves, even at the dinner table?

"Because it was weird how he picked on you yesterday, but then ended up being nice about it," says Logan.

Of course Logan doesn't know. I don't even know if Mr. Brumby is aware that we're going to be related... unless that's why he decided to be nice to me. Wait. Of course—that's why he called me *Pipsqueak*. He wasn't being demeaning. He was using the same nickname that Grandpa uses for me all the time. He was trying to tell me that he knew more things about me than a regular teacher. Grandpa must have told him about his granddaughter, including the intimate personal hormonal details. Oh misery. I'd rather Mr. Brumby was being demeaning.

Logan takes my hand. "I'm going to be late for my Spanish class. Will you talk to me when you figure things out?"

I nod my head, and Logan moves away, which is a lucky thing, because if he hadn't, I'd be crying right there in the hallway with nowhere to hide except deep in the back of my locker, which isn't as unrealistic an option for me as it is for normal-sized people. I take several slow breaths as I open my locker and hang up my jacket. If I want to arrive in class without being a sobbing mess, I know I have to distract myself. My photo of Brooklyn is taped to the inside door, and I touch his white nose with a fingertip. I am a fantastic unstoppable person. The unicorn's nose is quite similar to Brooklyn's, except for the horn. I'm likeable, and I try to do the right thing—despite what Taylor thinks. I'm not abusive. I'm so tired of her trying to convert me to her woo woo version of horsemanship that would prohibit riding, jumping and galloping. I gather my books and slam my locker door, which hits the wayward cuff of my jacket and immediately bounces open again. I feel like tearing the jacket off the hook and stomping it with my feet, but instead I tuck the sleeve back in place. What is the matter with Taylor? How can she be so dense? How could she believe that I wouldn't put Brooklyn first, ahead of everything else? She should know me better. Who does she think she is? I close the door more carefully, watching as Brooklyn's face slides slowly into the darkness.

Chapter Sixteen

A week goes by without much happening. Topaz's bald spot grows bigger, as does Kansas's tummy, which I would never have thought possible. The unicorn has been extremely obliging and stayed clear of my dreams. There's been no word from Grandpa; I've ridden my bike past the seniors village a few times, and the unit he and Isobel were looking at now sports a *SOLD* sticker, but whether they are the new owners or not, I have no way of knowing.

Mr. Brumby continues to be nice to me, which I find deeply troubling. Logan thinks it's hilarious and that doesn't help. Logan wants me to talk about it but I'd rather not; it's much easier to avoid spending time with Logan, and that is what I've been doing.

I signed up for the babysitting course, and it starts tomorrow. I was excited about it at first, but as the date has drawn closer, I've been less and less looking forward to it. Babysitting class is not going to be anywhere near as much fun as learning about horses and riding. Plus, there is a lot of responsibility. I have second thoughts about whether I'm ready for this, but my parents are so proud of me that I can't quit, and Dad has opened an investment account, where I can deposit all the money I earn. Plus, Kansas and Declan are counting on me. I'm still not crazy about changing diapers, but if I learn how to do baby CPR, I'll be able to save her life and that would be exciting.

I still haven't told my parents that Kansas's and Declan's baby has tested positive for Turner Syndrome. I'm not sure that Kansas wants me to keep the information confidential, but I know I want to keep it private for as long as possible. I like thinking about having a little sister. I like the idea of someone else being as short as I am. I like that I will be able to tell her things about being a Turner girl that no one else will know.

My mom is busy landing a new employee assistance contract for her office, so the fact that I am participating in a death-defying sport has disappeared from her agenda. I figure this is temporary, until my next event, when she will be back focusing her anxieties on me like a laser.

Meanwhile, I have been focused on maintaining Brooklyn's fitness for our next competition, which is a month away, and I can barely contain my excitement. Another cross-country! This time I hope to place in the ribbons, even though it won't be easy, what with Kansas being unable to do anything strenuous, and Taylor's unwillingness to groom. Whenever I've seen Taylor at the stables, she's been taking Spike off for a gentle meadow walk. I've been left to ride by myself, which is fine. I'm not really by myself; I'm with Brooklyn.

Brooklyn is stronger now than he's ever been. I've done a heap of online research about horse nutrition to be sure he's getting the right nutrients for the extra work he's doing.

His coat is gleaming, his muscles are rippling, and whenever I'm out of Kansas's sight I let him gallop faster than I've ever imagined. He seems pretty happy to me, despite what Taylor would say is my abusive, irresponsible behaviour. He lets me catch him every time when he's grazing out in the field, he never bites me, he doesn't pin his ears when I tighten the girth the way that Hambone does all the time to Kansas. I'd say life is pretty good.

Kansas still wants us to practice our dressage, though. We didn't do all that well in the dressage phase at the last event, so she's asked Declan to clear all the jumps out of the ring for several dedicated lessons on the flat. I try not to be ungrateful because I know she's right, and I know she enjoys teaching dressage more than anything else, but really it is a light-year beyond boring. There is zero excitement. It's all about the precision and accuracy of riding straight lines and circles. Plus there are points given for submission of the horse, which is somehow supposed to include harmony with the rider, and that is completely confusing for me, because how can there be harmony in a relationship where one has to submit to the other? Like math class, for example: Mr. Brumby can intimidate us into obedience, but it sure doesn't feel harmonious, not from my point of view.

Today we've warmed up at the walk and are just starting some twenty-metre trot circles when Kansas tells me to stop.

"He's short on the near hind," she tells me. I twist in the saddle and watch her run her hands slowly down his back leg. "There's heat here," she says when she reaches his hock.

Brooklyn hasn't been lame since the day I met him. I am devastated. "Maybe he'll work out of it," I say.

"What have you been doing with him? Any jumping?"

"Just trails," I say. And, I do not add, galloping on that part of the pasture you can't see from the house.

Kansas feels the hock on the right leg for comparison, then returns to the left. "It's definitely warm. And I think there's a bit of swelling. You should cold-hose him and give him a few days off."

"What about the event? I have to keep him in condition."

"You have to keep him sound. He may just be popping a bog spavin, which wouldn't necessarily be a big deal, but let's give him the benefit of the doubt. You don't fool around with hocks. We should have the vet out, but I know how your dad would not like that, so let's start with old-fashioned first aid and stall rest for a few days. Hambone had something like this happen to him and he turned out fine." She's walking towards the barn as she talks, planning out loud. "I'll have to change his diet... I'll free-feed him that low-sugar hay we brought in for Spike. He won't like it, but it'll stop him from eating the barn. We can reassess in a week. Come on, Sylvia." She beckons impatiently with a swing of her arm.

A week? I can't ride for a whole week? What am I going to do instead?

I slip out of the saddle and lead Brooklyn to the barn. He's not acting like there's anything wrong, but I can't help feeling panicky. I take off his tack, slip on his halter, and lead him back outside where Kansas is struggling to attach the hose to the tap at the hitching rail.

"I'll show you how to do this," she says. She adjusts the flow from the tap to a steady trickle and aims it at Brooklyn's hoof. He's fine with this part, but as soon as she moves it and the water hits skin, he bolts to the end of the lead rope as if he's been bitten by a snake.

"Oh for heaven's sake," says Kansas. "It's just a little water."

I stick my hand in it to check the temperature. "It's freezing cold," I say.

"It's supposed to be cold. Bring him back here and tie him up first, then we'll try again."

"I don't want to tie him up. What if he loses his mind and panics?" I'm so close to panicking myself that it makes twisted sense that Brooklyn is feeling the same way, even though he's not normally that kind of horse.

"Really, Sylvia, this is basic horsemanship, it's not a big deal. He has to learn how to do this without having a fit." She's exasperated, which is not a good way to be around horses. Usually she knows better. Hormones—ugh.

Taylor appears magically from out of the barn. I didn't even know she was here. She has a feed bucket in one hand and a grain scoop in the other. She walks up to Brooklyn whose nose immediately dives into the bucket, and she trickles in a few flakes of oats. "Now try the hose," she says, putting the bucket on the ground.

Brooklyn is so focused on the grain that he couldn't care less about the water.

"That's cheating," says Kansas.

"Oh yeah," says Taylor. "I prefer to think of it as *teaching.*"

"I don't believe in using bribery," says Kansas.

Taylor raises her eyebrows and considers Kansas's belly. "You might change your mind in a few weeks," says the babysitting expert.

Kansas ignores Taylor's comment and concentrates on gradually moving the stream of water up Brooklyn's leg until it flows around his hock joint. "Keep it here for fifteen minutes." She motions for me to hold the hose. "You two obviously don't need me, I'm going back in my house for a nap." She stomps off, leaving me alone with Taylor. Well, not alone, because Brooklyn is still there, munching away on miniscule bits of oats.

"I didn't know you were here," I say. I loop the lead rope over the hitching rail but don't bother to tie it because Brooklyn isn't interested in going anywhere else.

Taylor shrugs but doesn't say anything.

"Kansas says there's heat in his hock," I say, because I desperately need to talk about it.

"I wonder how that happened," says Taylor.

Since she hasn't bothered to make this into a question, I am not going to answer.

"You haven't replied to any of my emails," says Taylor. "I suppose you haven't read any of the links."

I'm not getting into that now, not when I'm so worried about Brooklyn. "Kansas says I can't ride him for a few days. If he doesn't get better quickly he'll lose condition and we won't be able to enter the next event."

"How devastating," says Taylor.

I loathe that Taylor is being sarcastic. I don't like it when anyone is sarcastic, but it's worse coming from Taylor, who is usually kind and gentle.

"It's my fault, isn't it? Because I've been letting him gallop."

Taylor gives Brooklyn three more oats. I move the hose to wet the other side of his hock. I will not cry.

Taylor digs into her back pocket and pulls out a package of gum. She hands me a stick and takes one for herself. We unwrap and chew.

"It's sugar-free," says Taylor.

"That's a relief," I say, attempting a small joke, because how could I worry about calories at a time like this? Taylor doesn't laugh. I adjust the hose so the water runs down the back of Brooklyn's hock and drips off his fetlock into the gravel.

"You can't be a carefree kid forever," says Taylor.

Carefree? Does she not know how much I have to worry about?

"You have to step up and take responsibility," she continues.

What is she talking about? "I've signed up for the baby-sitting course," I say.

"That's not what I mean," says Taylor. "You have to take responsibility for your horse's long-term well-being."

I check my watch. "Five more minutes to go," I say. I will not look at her, I don't care what she says, not if she's getting into that spiritual horsemanship stuff again.

She is quiet for three whole minutes (I timed her).

"It's not just about the horse," says Taylor. "As much as you complain about being patronized because you're short, you're acting as though you prefer to stay a little kid. You scoot along under everyone's radar, not taking a stand. It's like you're choosing to not grow up."

La la la la la, I am not listening. I am thinking my own thoughts and not paying attention. I sing to myself Helen Austin's *Always be a Unicorn* song. "*Always be yourself...*"

"I know you're supposed to be starting hormone treatment, Sylvia. Your mom is really worried and blabs to my mom about it all the time. I know your mom promised that you could decide when to start on your own, but time's running out. You're almost fifteen. You're not talking about it; I bet you're not even thinking about it. You're putting it off, just like you put off being responsible for Brooklyn; you only want to live in the moment and have fun. Like a kid. Forever."

I am so shocked I can hardly breathe. This is not any of her business. This is personal and private. This is a no-go zone. There are red flags all over the place. Who does she think she is?

And I know it's immature, I know, I know, but I can't help myself, I take that hose and press my thumb across the open end, and I aim the stream of pressurized water right at her head.

Chapter Seventeen

Taylor screams, drops the bucket and the grain scoop. Oats fly everywhere.

Brooklyn takes off across the yard, ripping the hose out of my hands as he passes. He trots down .the driveway dragging his lead rope, nostrils flaring, tail in the air like a flagpole. The horses in the pasture catch the excitement and gallop in a huge circle before heading straight to the fence nearest Brooklyn. Over the thunder of hooves, I can hear Bernadette barking her head off in Kansas's house.

"Is the gate closed? The one on the driveway?" I say. I can't remember if I closed it, or if Taylor came in after me and closed it herself. If Brooklyn escapes onto the road, he could be mushed by a truck, or put his feet through the windshield of a sports car and kill all the occupants. I'd be sued, Kansas would be sued, and worse yet, I'd never again have a horse to ride.

The gate is not visible from the barn, so I follow Brooklyn's path at a run even though I know that chasing loose horses makes them feel pursued so their instincts as prey animals kick in, and they run even faster.

I'm halfway down the driveway before I can see that the gate is shut, and Brooklyn has found a patch of grass in front of it. His head is down, munching, but the tension remains in his body: he is holding his tail out from his buttocks, and he tears at the grass with short, fierce bites. I force myself to slow to a walk and call to him gently. I tell him he's a good boy and that this would be a great time to whoa and stand.

Hambone pushes the herd into a corner on the far side of the pasture, and all seems peaceful until I'm within a few metres of Brooklyn, and that's when Hambone breaks from the herd, and ears pinned and teeth bared, takes a direct run at him. He puts on the brakes at the last minute and slides chest-first into the fence. Brooklyn wheels away and prepares to trot past me on his way back to the barn. He's carrying his head to the left so he can keep an eye on the lead rope snaking along beside him.

"Brooklyn, whoa!" I spread my arms to take up more space on the driveway. Usually, when I collect Brooklyn from the pasture, he trots right up to me as soon as he sees me, and I'm hoping this will happen. It's not until the last second that I see I've been kidding myself. Brooklyn dekes onto the grass verge, breaks into a canter beside me and kicks out his back feet. I feel a gust of wind cross my fingers.

It's bad enough that he didn't whoa when I told him to, and that he didn't stop when my body language made it very clear that I wanted him to. But his threatening to kick me is devastating. Why would he do such a thing? He could have killed me. I check my hand. The skin has been torn clear off one knuckle. It happened so fast I hardly felt a thing. If he'd kicked me in the head, I'd be dead. Brooklyn, who I love, has almost killed me. And I thought he loved me.

By the time I've walked back to the barn, I'm ready to beat him. I've never felt like this before in my life—betrayed and angry and frightened. I'm seething with a hot urge to inflict pain.

Taylor has collected my horse. They are standing beside the hitching rail, and she is allowing him to nose through the spilled oats in the gravel.

"Don't reward him," I say. "He tried to kick me." I grab for the lead rope, but Taylor swings it up and out of my reach.

"If he meant to kick you, you would have been kicked. Horses always know precisely where their feet are," says Taylor.

I hold up my bleeding finger as evidence.

"Yikes," she says. "That was close."

My finger is trembling, as are my hand, my arm, and everything else.

"Let me put him in his stall for you," says Taylor. She leads him away.

The hose is still running. I use it to rinse my hand, then shut off the tap. I blot my knuckle on my shirt, leaving a pattern like small red flowers. I don't like blood. It better wash out. I hope my mom doesn't interrogate me about what happened, I'll have to lie, I don't want her to know that Brooklyn can be dangerous on the ground, without getting on his back and jumping colossal cross-country fences. I don't want to believe it myself.

Taylor returns from the barn and leans against the hitching rail. "I'm sorry I upset you," she says. She tucks some wet hair behind her ear. Her t-shirt is wet in a U-shape across her shoulders and down to her waist. It clings to her, revealing her shape, the one I'm not sure I want to have.

She notices me staring, and somehow she understands. "It's not so bad being a girl," she says.

"I am a girl."

"You know what I mean," says Taylor.

And I do know. But it's personal and private and I am not going to talk about it.

"Topaz has trichotillomania," I say. "She pulls out her hairs, one at a time. She's got a bald spot." I stick the toe of my boot into the gravel and water runs in to fill the depression.

"Whatever you say," says Taylor.

I hear her footsteps as she walks around to the other side of the barn to visit Spike's paddock. I won't watch her and her swaying curves. After a moment, I make my way to Brooklyn's stall. I unlatch his door and step in. Taylor has given him a flake of Spike's low-sugar hay, which looks like straw. Kansas says it would taste like Styrofoam, but it's the only way to manage Spike's thrifty metabolism. Brooklyn is poking away at it as though nothing has happened. He flips the hay with his nose, then searches the floor beneath for something more palatable. He doesn't look up when I enter but I can see his eye so I know he has seen me.

"I'm not going to hurt you," I tell him, "not now." I approach him warily and he moves his hip away from me as I draw closer. "I should check your leg. If you were lame before, you're probably extra lame now." I press my body against his hind leg, the way Kansas has shown me, because there's less chance of being hurt if you're close against the horse. I don't now why I've remembered this; it certainly wasn't relevant when she told me. I thought she was being overly cautious, as usual. She's been going on and on about how unpredictable and dangerous horses can be since the moment I met her. It didn't make sense until today.

I hold my hand over his injured hock, and compare the

heat to the other leg. I can't feel any difference. I don't have the sense of touch that Kansas has. I can't see the swelling either. Both hocks look equally bumpy and lumpy. I have no eye for this.

What will I do with myself if I can't ride for a week? Or six weeks? Or forever? If Brooklyn is permanently lame, I don't think Grandpa will buy me another horse, not if he and Isobel are financing a new home. And my parents are already questioning the suitability of equestrian sports—losing Brooklyn would be convenient from their point of view. I'd have to wait until I'm older, with my own job, and lots of money saved before I could ride again. It's nothing short of tragic.

I leave the barn under a cloud of gloom and pedal my bike home.

Chapter Eighteen

It's Friday night, which is date night for Mom and Dad. They dress up, eat dinner somewhere fancy, and then go dancing or take in a movie. They've already left by the time I get home. I can smell Mom's perfume in the entranceway, which makes me miss her a little bit. The house feels big and empty.

I strip off my blood-splattered shirt and throw it in the washer along with a bunch of other clothes waiting in the laundry hamper. I add a scoop of soap powder and set the machine to work.

As part of the deal with date night, I can eat whatever I want for dinner. I fry myself a grilled cheese sandwich with mayo and pickles. I make the best grilled cheese in the world, because I fry with butter at a low temperature, which means that the bread turns golden brown at the exact same moment as the cheese melts to perfection. I use real cheddar (not the single cheese slices, which taste like plastic), and crisp sweet pickles, and eat it all up while it's warm.

As good as this is, there's something even better about

date night. I have unlimited access to the computer, with no one around to worry that I'm going to become an Internet addict or destroy my melatonin levels by watching a blue screen, or make inappropriate connections on social media. Bliss. I can go anywhere on the web as long as I remember to delete the browser history file before I head to bed (I learned this the hard way when I was younger).

First, I read about hock injuries and bog spavins. Some sites say that bog spavins are very common soft swellings on the joint surface; they are often no more than cosmetic in nature, cause little or no lameness, and respond well to rest. Maybe I should be satisfied with this, but instead I keep reading, and the more I read, the more terrified I feel, especially when I discover the sites sponsored by veterinary clinics, because all of these say how essential it is to consult a veterinarian to determine the exact problem and administer injections.

There are pages and pages of information with different opinions and treatment protocols.

In the end, I decide the best thing for me to do is to trust Kansas.

Next, I read up on feeding strategies. I wasn't happy to hear about Brooklyn having to eat Spike's hay. The Internet pages on horse nutrition problems are at least as scary as the pages about joint injuries. Underfed horses don't perform well, but overfed horses can die, and sometimes horses colic and die no matter what they are fed.

I decide to leave this to Kansas as well.

I don't know if I have enough brain space to be a responsible horse owner and prevent all the terrible things that can happen to these animals at the drop of a hat.

I'm amazed how Kansas can manage a stable, where every horse has individual requirements that, if not properly met, can result in a huge dead body. At the same time, she has her baby to plan for, and yet she can't really plan until she knows which special blend of Turner Syndrome characteristics her baby pops out with. Kansas has to be ready for everything.

I leave the Google search screen and open my favourite horse-related Internet discussion forum. It's always good for some entertainment and education, and it's nice to feel connected to a bunch of like-minded horse nuts. There are some things that only horse people understand. I cruise around for a while. I don't participate. I prefer to lurk anonymously and observe. Someone named *OmegaMare* has posted selfies with her gelding because she's dyed her hair to match his mane. *TwoTrickPonies* asks how to discourage her mare from peeing in her stall. *GalUp* is virtual horse shopping, and wants to hear from anyone who has had experience buying Lusitanos from a breeder in Brazil; she posts a link and I click it. Lusitanos look like larger versions of Brooklyn, with more magnificent noses. Maybe I will go to Brazil when Brooklyn is old and buy one for myself.

I wonder what I would post about if I was going to post—which I am not. Maybe I'd want to know if there were any horse people who were also Turner girls. That might be interesting.

I've never met anyone else with TS, in the real world or the virtual world. My mom offered to take me to a conference about Turners in Vancouver, but since everyone with Turners has their own peculiar range of symptoms, I wasn't sure there was a point to going. Besides, Mom was concerned about my self-identifying with a syndrome—she said there was a lot more to me than having TS. And Dad said that hotels were ridiculously expensive in Vancouver. So we didn't go, and I guess it worked out for the best, but sometimes I still have a faint hankering to meet someone else with TS. I can't explain why.

I leave the forum and cruise through a list of Turners sites. I know better than to open the medical ones. I look for a blog, or a discussion group, and nothing strikes my fancy. I switch to Facebook. A search reveals several groups for people interested in Turner Syndrome. They're all closed. I can't lurk. If I want to see the posts, I have to join a group. I'd have to step out from under the radar. One group is for *Turner Syndrome Sistas*. I like the sound of that one and open the page. I slide the cursor over the *Join Group* button. My finger hovers.

Outside I hear voices. Mom and Dad are home.

My finger plunges of its own accord.

I have joined the Sistas.

Quickly, I erase the browser history. Not that I've done anything wrong, but Mom will look, and her imagination will run wild, she'll think I've been worrying too much about my horse and my self and that I have an anxiety disorder and will need therapy or medication. I dash to the bathroom, where I'm calmly brushing my teeth when Mom and Dad come down the hall, smiling and laughing. They've had a good night. So have I.

Chapter Nineteen

I dream about the unicorn again. This time it's no accident. When the dream started, I was in the alleyway of Kansas's barn. At first, I thought I'd like to spend some time with Brooklyn, but I remembered that our relationship, along with his leg, was a bit strained. So I conjured up the unicorn instead.

His horn is twisted in a ridiculous rainbow.

"How do you like my new look?" he says, turning his head so his horn catches the light. A stripe of gold gleams brightly.

"I didn't think you were the attention-seeking type," I say.

He snuffs. "You're right, I'm not. This has nothing to do with seeking attention and everything to do with self expression."

I don't know what to say to that.

"It's not easy being a unicorn," he says. "There are so few of us. It would be much easier to be a horse. And speaking of oddness, how's your life going?"

Oddness? He thinks I'm odd? I might argue the point if I

didn't have bigger problems weighing on me. "Not great," I say. "I may have lamed my horse. Everyone's upset with me, except for Grandpa, and he's so far away, it hardly counts."

"Don't worry about the horse. He needs a week of rest and cold-water treatment, then a gradual return to exercise. He'll be fine."

"Even a veterinarian would need x-rays to know that for sure."

"You caught it early, and other than the unfortunate extra activity this afternoon, you've treated it properly. I have special powers in this regard," says the unicorn. "And you have a more important matter to deal with. This break in training gives you the perfect opportunity to attend to it. And you know exactly what it is."

I could easily wake myself up. All I'd have to do is turn my head an inch on the pillow.

"Wait a minute," says the unicorn. "There's something I want you to hear."

With difficulty, I conjure some patience.

"Believe it or not," he continues, "for a long time I struggled with being a unicorn. Because there are so few of us, and because we're not herd animals, there aren't many accessible role models. This meant decision-making could be terribly challenging. Choices that might be right for some creatures wouldn't necessarily be right for me."

I nod to indicate I'm listening, but really he is so self-absorbed I can hardly concentrate.

"Now I look differently at my life. I think less about the difficulties of being a unicorn, and more about what I, as a singularity, get to do."

He stops and stares at me expectantly. I do nothing.

"Alright, this would be a better time for you to wake yourself up," he says.

"Wait a minute. What has this to do with me? I'm thinking—I'm not ready for this dream to finish."

"Even so," says the unicorn, and he trots towards me, rainbow horn lowered and aimed at one side of my chest.

I stand my ground. I will sleep as long as I want to, I am in charge here, that's the way it works with lucid dreams.

He pokes me and I wake up.

There is a tender spot over top of my heart. I rub it until I fall back to sleep.

Usually on Saturday mornings I'm so excited about spending the day at the barn that I'm out of the house by nine. Today, I'm slouching around in my tartan pyjamas, sneaking some extra computer time before Mom and Dad get up. I have a notice from Facebook that I've been accepted into the *Turner Syndrome Sistas* group. I open the group page. Facebook wants me to write something, so I do. "I have TS. I'm turning 15 and live on Vancouver Island. I don't know anyone else with TS." I hit the Post button before I can talk myself out of it.

The doorbell rings. At nine on a Saturday morning. This is unheard of. I open the door, and there is Logan Losino. His hair is flattened, and he's holding a helmet under his arm. Leaning against our front steps is his full-suspension mountain bike that he's really proud of, as if it's alive.

And I'm in my PJs. And my hair hasn't been brushed at all. Nor have my teeth. I'm wearing the stupid rabbit slippers that my parents gave me for Christmas; they're still buying inappropriate clothes for me from the children's department because they fit, and I only wear them because they are comfortable. Why did I open the door?

"You want to go for a bike ride?" says Logan, as though I look perfectly normal, as though it's acceptable for someone who is almost fifteen to wear clothes designed for eight-year-olds.

"I'd have to change," I say.

"You think?" says Logan. He can make jokes about anything. He looks at the slippers. "My mom would love those," he says.

Logan's never been to my house before. Usually, we hang out at school. I don't know what to do with him. I'm not taking him to my room, that's for sure. I haven't made my bed, and I need privacy to change. But if I leave him in the kitchen, there's a risk my parents will stumble across him. My dad might think he's an intruder and hit him over the head with the fire extinguisher. Or my mom would make his visit into a socially momentous event that I'd never hear the end of. "Would you mind waiting outside?" I say. "I'll be five minutes."

"Sure," says Logan, as though this is perfectly normal too. Maybe it is.

I change and brush up in record time, then leave a note on the kitchen table telling my parents I've left for the barn.

My bike is nothing special like Logan's. He uses his in competitions, and I use mine to get to school or the barn. I have to pedal hard, and Logan coasts along.

"Where are we going?" says Logan.

"I have to treat Brooklyn's leg," I say. "After that we can do whatever we want for a while, until my babysitting course later this afternoon."

"That's fantastic," says Logan. He's happy because he knows that all of my spare time is usually spent at the barn. I haven't encouraged him to visit me there because he'd be bored to death watching me ride in the ring, and although he could accompany us on his bike on trail rides, I don't want to share my Brooklyn time. I don't want to have to talk to anyone. I like being with Brooklyn, communicating with a shift of weight or a word or sometimes just a thought. And he communicates back to me with the flick of an ear, a new angle to his neck, or a change of pace. It's a delicate conversation. I like Logan more than most people, but still... I like to ride my horse. By myself.

Today is different though, because I won't be riding at all. This will make it a special day for Logan, and something of a drag for me.

I tell him about Brooklyn's bog spavin, and about how I can't ride for at least a week, and I don't know how I'm going to stand it. Unfortunately, this reminds me of what the unicorn told me about using this time as an opportunity. I don't think so. I pedal faster, and faster. I want to leave everything behind, including Logan, but he catches up and stays beside me.

"What's the hurry?" he says. "Where's the fire?" He laughs, stands high above his saddle and pushes his pedals like crazy, zooming far ahead of me. He does figure-eights in the middle of the road until I catch up. What a show-off.

I don't talk to him as we pass shoulder to shoulder, with Logan going back in the direction I've come from. "Wait for meeeeee!" he says.

I pedal as hard as I can, but in seconds he's caught up with me again.

"Are you okay?" he says. "Because you look kind of angry."

"I'm not angry," I say automatically, then realize that I am.

He pedals ahead of me and stops at an angle across my path. I have to stop too, unless I want to run over him, which wouldn't be such a bad idea if it was even remotely possible for my wimpy little kid's bike to take on his ultra-strong metal monster.

"Do you not like me any more?" says Logan. "Because

you're not talking to me at school, and you don't seem very happy right now either."

I'm puffing and it takes a minute to catch my breath, which is fine because this gives me time to think of something to say. Of course I still like him, he is one of the few people who likes me the way I am, what would my life be like without Logan Losino? What's the matter with him? What I don't need right now is more relationship pressure. I like him, but I'm mad at him. What a mess.

"You've changed," says Logan, sticking a dagger in my heart.

I want to say, "Not as much as I'm going to! And I'm terrified!" But I can't. My eyes are all wet and spill onto my cheeks. I wipe my face on my sleeve. "It's from the wind," I mumble. "The same thing happens when I gallop."

"What?" says Logan.

This is way too much trouble. I cannot figure myself out, let alone explain myself to someone else. "I'll see you at school," I say, edging my bike around his. I don't look back. I am unstoppable, even when I don't necessarily want to be.

Chapter Twenty

Kansas is scrubbing out water tubs when I arrive at the barn. It's not a fun job at the best of times, and she's struggling to keep her balance while reaching down and around the equivalent of a basketball strapped to her belly. When I first met her she was slim and almost boy-like. It was one of the things I liked about her. Now, she looks deformed, like a total exaggeration of womanhood. I don't know how she can stand it.

"Oh, am I glad to see you," says Kansas.

"Good," I say. I will not cry in front of Kansas. She has enough to worry about. "How's the baby?" I ask.

She pats her belly. "She's kicking the stall walls this morning."

I grab a brush and the last tub and set to scrubbing beside her.

Kansas is wearing a pale yellow maternity smock with little puffed sleeves embroidered at the edges. It's wet and filthy. Before Kansas was pregnant her favourite barn clothes were jeans, men's work shirts, and rubber boots, mostly from the second-hand stores. Probably her maternity clothes are second-hand as well; they sure don't look like anything she'd buy new for herself, even if there were a maternity section in Work Wear World. Her arms are wet and dirty, and there is dirt under her nails. Mostly, ever since Kansas has been pregnant, I've been noticing how she's changed, what with the mood swings and the physical developments. It's a relief to notice some things are the same. Underneath it all, she's still my Kansas who likes hanging around with horses and doesn't care about staying clean .

"I've been reading everything I can put my hands on about Turner Syndrome," she says. "I know you've told me stuff before, but most of it didn't sink in, I'm sorry to admit. I'm balanced by seeing you, and how normal you are; otherwise I'd drive myself crazy with all the potential problems. Worrying is a waste of time—I understand that. We won't know for sure what we have to deal with until she's born."

"Or even later," I say, thinking of the estrogen patches hidden in the back of my drawer. I'm flattered that Kansas thinks I'm normal, and at the same time I feel uncomfortable that I've misled her.

Kansas attaches a nozzle to the hose and spray cleans each tub. I'm reminded of how I sprayed Taylor in the face. I feel bad. Taylor was only trying to help.

We put a tub in each stall, open the taps and supervise the filling.

"On days like today, I wish I'd put in automatic waterers," says Kansas from the next stall. "But I wouldn't have been able to monitor the horses' water intake, and the lines freeze in the winter time... "

I hear the fatigue in her voice. She has all these horses to take care of, and now she's having a baby, a Turner baby, and who knows how much extra work that is going to be.

"My mother wants to move out here so she can help, which is ironic given that she was on the team that didn't want us to keep the baby after we heard the test results."

The water fills the tub at my feet and a large eddy swirls on the surface.

"She wanted you to give up your baby for adoption?" I say.

There is a very long pause before Kansas answers. "No. She wanted us to terminate. Sorry, I wasn't going to tell you. I probably shouldn't have."

I hear Kansas shut off her tap and leave the stall. She peers in at me. "You okay?"

"It's kind of weird, what you just said," I say. "I knew there was a higher risk of miscarrying a Turners baby, but I didn't know... " It is too much to say. My parents didn't figure out that I had TS until last year, but I wonder if they had known before I was born whether they would have kept me. I try to imagine not being born, and the world without me. Creepy.

Kansas says, "Between the risk of miscarriage and the option of termination, any Turner girl who survives has to be some sort of miracle, wouldn't you say, Sylvia?"

I turn off the tap. Kansas is wonderful. Just like that, she's helped me change from feeling that I'm worthless to believing that I'm ultra special.

"What are you going to do about your mom?" I say.

Kansas grimaces. "I don't know. Any time I'm around her, I regress to childhood. I don't imagine that would be good for my baby." She grabs another water tub and hauls it into Hambone's stall. I hear the tap open. I take a tub into Brooklyn's stall.

"I think you'll be a wonderful mother," I say, speaking loud enough for her to hear me down the alleyway and over the sound of running water.

"She wants to live in the travel trailer now that we've moved into the house," says Kansas. "I'm trying to discourage her without hurting her feelings. It would be nice to have some help, but I can't imagine it working. She's used to more space. *I'm* used to more space."

"I know what you mean," I say. "My mom is always barging in on my space. Even when she says she's going to leave something totally to me, she doesn't. She promised that starting hormone treatment was completely my decision, but she sneaks into my room and looks at the box of estrogen patches to see if one is missing." I'm talking about it. I'm actually talking about it. I can't believe it.

"That is a drag," says Kansas.

"I don't know if I want to be a woman," I say. "I mean a developed one."

"Could you see yourself as a man instead?"

"Ha!" I say. "No, that's not what I mean at all. It's just that what happens inside is so private and personal. And then when you develop, everybody can notice."

"Tell me about it," says Kansas. "I was never into flaunting myself either, but now everything's on display, whether I like it or not. And total strangers remark on it, as though being pregnant makes my body public property. It drives me nuts."

This gives me something to think about. I'd assumed that Kansas didn't mind looking the way she did. I'd assumed she was, if not exactly attention-seeking, at least something close to it. Instead, it's more a case of begrudging attention acceptance.

"That's what I'm afraid will happen when I start taking estrogen," I say. "People will notice and make comments. I don't want them to make comments, even good ones."

"You know, I remember feeling that way when I was around your age," says Kansas. "I'd forgotten... but I was the same. My mom was always pushing me to wear revealing feminine clothing, but I was mortified if my bra strap showed."

"You mean it's normal to feel like this?" I say. "It's not because I have Turners?"

"That would be it—completely normal, just like me," says Kansas, laughing. She has finished Hambone's stall and is standing in Brooklyn's open doorway. "And from what I've been reading about Turners, it sounds like there are advantages to taking estrogen, other than obtaining wanton womanly characteristics. Estrogen is good for your bone health— and strong bones would make you a better rider. At least there'd be lower risk of fractures from those unscheduled dismounts."

"I've read about that... but I forgot," I say.

Kansas wipes her hands dry on her smock, then wrings the fabric to rid it of water. There's a ripping sound, and when she flattens the smock over her belly there's a ragged tear across the middle. "I'll be so glad when I can get out of this flimsy crap and back into real clothes," says Kansas.

"I've been worried about more than physical changes. I'm afraid my brain will be different too."

"Maybe you'll change and be even better," says Kansas. "I did read about estrogen improving non-verbal skills in Turner girls."

"Do you think estrogen could make me better at math?"

Before she can answer there's a loud *Yoo Hoo* from the end of the alleyway. A thin figure is silhouetted against the sunlit opening; a suitcase stands squarely beside her. Through the tack room window, I see a taxi departing down the driveway—with all the noise from running water, we hadn't heard it arrive.

"I always know I can find you in the barn," says the figure.

"Mom?" says Kansas.

"Surprise!"

"Lord, give me strength," says Kansas under her breath.

"I'm sorry," says Kansas's mom flitting towards us, "it was a spontaneous decision, but the closer I came the less sure it seemed like a good idea. I know I should have warned you, but I also knew you'd never ask for help, no matter how much you needed it, and if I said I wanted to come you'd tell me I shouldn't trouble myself, but on the other hand—"

"Mom, it's okay," says Kansas, holding out her arms. "It's good to see you."

They hug, awkwardly, around the beach ball.

"Are you sure it's okay, Kansas? And Declan won't mind? I know how independent you are."

"It's fine," says Kansas. She is an expert liar. "And I'd like you to meet my friend and stable helper, Sylvia. Sylvia, this is my mother, Ida."

I hold out my hand for her to shake, but she whips right past it and hugs me. I have a nanosecond to decide whether to hug her back or not: this is the person who suggested that Kansas terminate a pregnancy because of a Turner Syndrome diagnosis, but she's also Kansas's mom. And she doesn't seem too bad. I close my arms around her waist as she squeezes me into her belly, apparently not caring that I'm filthy and missing a chromosome.

Chapter Twenty-One

I hose Brooklyn's leg all by myself because Kansas wants to help her mom settle in the travel trailer before Declan comes home from work. Then I ride my bike home and change my clothes, because it's probably not appropriate to wear dirty wet jeans and t-shirt to a babysitting class. I scrub my hands too.

I haven't been looking forward to the class, so it's not as though my expectations are high, but still I am deeply disappointed as soon as I open the classroom door, because the first thing I see is Topaz, and the second thing I see is that the only empty seat is the one right beside her.

She's playing with her hair when I sit down.

"Hey, Topaz," I say.

"Oh. It's you," she says.

Nice start.

"I thought you were too busy with your horse to have time for babysitting," says Topaz.

"A friend of mine is pregnant," I say. "I want to be able

to help her out. I need to learn how to do baby First Aid and CPR. Why are you here?"

"I need to start making money so I can move out," she says. She's brought a notebook with her and she's filling the first page with squiggles and doodles. She is not what I would call artistic.

"That will be a lot of babysitting," I say. My dad has done a thorough job of explaining to me how long it takes to save money, even if you're not spending it on essential equestrian gear.

Topaz shrugs. "I have to get out. Amber is going to make my life impossible."

"Amber already makes my life impossible," I say.

"This is different. It's about her boyfriend, Franco. A secret."

She wouldn't be telling me this if she remembered that Franco is Logan's brother. Everyone forgets, because they look more like they come from different species than the same family.

"Oh, I know all about Franco," I say. "He used to date my cousin Taylor. As a matter of fact, he was still dating Taylor when I caught him cheating with Amber. He wanted that kept a secret too, but I didn't. I told Taylor and then she broke up with him."

"Franco told me that he broke up with Taylor. And now he wants to break up with Amber. He wants to move on to better things, but he says Amber is too fragile." She prints his name on her page, then draws dagger lines through it until the letters disappear under a mass of ink.

I snort. "Amber? Fragile?"

"He thinks he's god's gift to women," says Topaz.

I remember my mom telling me that Topaz must be deeply unhappy if she's pulling out her own hair. That's certainly how she looks, squashed into her chair, destroying a piece of paper, her hair a squirrely mess. She hasn't always looked like this. She used to be more normal. Not that I know anything about what normal is. For all I know, it's normal for teenage girls to look pathetic. I don't have a chance to discuss this thought with her unfortunately because our instructor arrives. We spend an hour learning not about baby CPR, as I'd hoped, but about the business of babysitting: how to schedule appointments; how to list emergency contacts; rates to charge and how to calculate how much is owed. If it doesn't get more interesting than this, I'll be in a coma by the end of the course.

Topaz scuttles away quickly at the end of the hour and I ride my bike home. Dad is cooking dinner and Mom is reading in the living room. I go to my room and shut the door.

I open the drawer of my dresser and find the box of estrogen patches. Each patch is wrapped in its own protective pouch. I've never opened one. When Mom gave me the box she was over-the-moon excited and expected me to be excited too. At last I could catch up with my classmates, she told me. I could be like everyone else! As if that would be a good thing, to be anything at all like Amber. Or Topaz.

Since promising she wouldn't pressure me, I'm amazed she's kept her word—she's never been able to in the past. Sometimes it seems like she has interfered with my life from the moment I was born.

I put the packet back in the box and the box back in the drawer, draping the toe of a black sock just so over one corner.

I'm almost ready, but not quite.

Maybe after dinner.

Dad is yelling from the kitchen that my food is on the

table. It's always best to be prompt on the nights that Dad cooks.

He's made his special lamb soup, with chick peas and cilantro and I don't know what else.

We all take our seats. Mom has a sip of soup.

"Tony, what spices do you use in this recipe?" she says.

"If I told you my secret ingredients, they wouldn't be secret any more," says Dad.

"Have it your way," says Mom.

"This is delicious, Dad," I say. I'm not crazy about the idea of eating cute little baby sheep, and usually I find lamb flavour too strong, and then there was that unpleasant episode with Amber bah-ing at me at school... but even I have to admit this soup is fantastic.

Dad flutters a hand. "Oh, it was nothing."

I glance at Mom, and she forces a small smile. "You should cook more often, Tony."

I could see where this was headed from the other side of the universe.

"Kansas's mom arrived today," I say quickly.

"That will be nice for Kansas to have some help with the baby," says Mom.

"It was a surprise," I say.

"They didn't know she was coming?" says Mom. "The behaviour of some people is quite incomprehensible."

I was hoping she'd react more favourably, given the upcoming surprise she has in store from Grandpa and Isobel.

"What do you think, Dad?" Normally, I can count on Dad to take any position not supported by Mom.

"In-laws are always incomprehensible," he says.

"But it's nice for families to be close and to support each other, don't you think?" If I don't convince them to see this in a more positive light, Grandpa is going to be in big trouble.

"Of course it is, Pumpkin," says Mom. "But people still have to respect each other's boundaries."

Dad snorts. We've heard the *boundaries* lecture many many times. "Ah yes, the psychological science of imaginary lines."

"No less imaginary than the *science* of economics," says Mom. "Now there's a load of self-serving crap if I ever heard one." Yikes. She's feisty today. Usually, she's in a better mood on the nights she doesn't have to cook.

"I'd like it if Grandpa lived closer," I say.

"Evie, you took one entry-level economics course at university. This hardly qualifies you to question modern economic theory," says Dad.

"And yet you can mock me, when you took zero psychology courses," says Mom.

"Kansas had prenatal genetic testing. They think her baby has Turner Syndrome," I say. I have given up the secret I was treasuring inside myself.

My parents both put down their spoons. Mom pats her lips with her napkin. Dad takes off his glasses and rubs his face with both hands.

"She doesn't need cardiac surgery because the prenatal echocardiogram showed her heart is fine," I say, because they seem to have taken my good news as a tragedy.

"Oh, dear lord," says Mom.

"It's not all bad. I feel like I'm going to have a little sister," I say. Surely my cheerfulness will count for something.

"Well, I hope they have extended health insurance to cover the prescription costs," says Dad.

I expect Mom to erupt about Dad focusing, yet again, on financial matters, but she doesn't. "They're already struggling.

You've seen how Kansas dresses. Everything is second-hand."

"No, Mom, she doesn't buy new clothes as a matter of principle. She likes—"

"I could look into insurance for them, Ev," says Dad. "I know a great broker."

"That's a good idea," says Mom. "They will need a lot of support. They're very young. Having a baby is challenging enough."

"It's not so bad!" I say. "They could have someone like me!"

They're staring at each other over the length of the table and don't hear a word I'm saying.

"You can offer lots of support, Ev," says Dad. "You are well trained and experienced."

Although it's nice that they're being kind to each other for a change, it's also a bit creepy. And their ignoring what I have to say leaves me feeling invisible as well as confused. I slide out of my chair and leave the table. No one tells me to stay and finish my dinner. I look back from the doorway, and they are both staring blankly out the window. A car drives by. A dog comes out of nowhere, lifts its leg, pees on our lamppost and runs away. Usually, this would make Dad mad, but he says nothing.

I don't understand this at all. What's the big deal?

I slip off to my bedroom and close the door behind me.

Chapter Twenty-Two

I stand in front of my mirror and confirm that I have not, in fact, become invisible. I point a finger at my reflection. "You are an unstoppable fantastic individual."

I raise my arms and flex my biceps. "You are an athlete."

I furrow my brow. "You have faced danger before."

Oh, what's the point? It's not me that needs convincing. I collapse backwards in a dejected heap on my bed. I'm tired of being treated like a kid or, worse still, like I'm not even here. I'm tired of being confused by my parents and... everyone else. But maybe the problem isn't with them. Maybe the problem is with me, and I don't understand because I still have a kid brain. Perhaps I'm the one who has to change.

I sit up. I can do that. I can change. It's not something I have to do; it's something I get to do. I can give my brain estrogen.

The time has arrived.

I take the box out of my dresser drawer, open it and remove a pouch. I read the instruction leaflet again. I've read it four thousand times already, but this time I need to be sure. I unzip my jeans and expose my butt. I stand in front of the mirror and look for a likely spot, away from my waistband, away from anywhere that might be rubbed by clothing. I tear the pouch, take out the patch and slap it on, pressing the edges firmly because it has to stay on for a whole week. I wrap the empty pouch in some tissues and toss the ball into my wastepaper basket. Then I zip up my jeans and sit back on the bed.

I wait to feel something. An itching where the estrogen meets my skin. A warmth where it penetrates to my blood. A rippling wave as it travels throughout my body. A burst of enlightenment when it reaches my brain.

Ten minutes pass. I feel nothing.

I put the box back in the drawer. I consider leaving it on top of the dresser. I know Mom is going to discover the missing pouch either way, but if I leave it in sight she may take it as a sign that I'm ready to talk about it with her, and I'm not.

I wonder if people will be able to tell by looking at me that I now have estrogen in my system.

I open my door and wander back to the kitchen. Mom and Dad are loading the dishwasher together. Usually, I do this job all by myself; it doesn't need two pairs of hands. They are talking quietly, and I can barely hear them. I'm in the shadow of the hallway, and they don't know I'm there. I hold myself still and lean against the wall.

"Do you think it would be easier to know from before birth?" says Mom. "Easier than how we found out, fourteen years too late?"

"Not too late," says Dad. "She's fine. We found out in time to help her."

"Can you imagine what it would have been like if we'd

known from the beginning? We would have been watching her like a hawk."

"You watched like a hawk as it was," says Dad. "You were a good mother."

Mom leans her head on his shoulder, and Dad puts his arm around her.

"I still feel guilty about having missed all the signs," says Mom. "She should have been diagnosed sooner."

"We both missed them," says Dad. "But she's fine. She's a great kid."

A cramp takes hold in my throat and there's pressure behind my eyes.

"We were lucky—" says Mom.

There. They've both got it now.

"It could have been much worse," she continues.

Worse? Wait a minute.

"All those problems she might have had, with her hearing, her heart, her kidneys... "

"There's no sense going down that road," says Dad.

"No, of course not. But Kansas and Declan may be heading down it."

Mom grabs a tissue and blows her nose, then loads three glasses in the washer. She puts them in the wrong place. Dad always corrects me if he sees me doing this, but he doesn't say anything to Mom.

"I'll see if I can find them some health insurance," says Dad.

And I'm going to learn baby First Aid and CPR. Everyone can relax when that's happened.

Mom says, "I wish Sylvie would start the estrogen. You don't suppose she's transgendered do you, and she doesn't want female characteristics because she'd be more comfortable as a boy? Have we been pushing too hard? Have we missed something else?"

"Oh, Evie," Dad croons. He kisses the top of her head.

"I don't mind if she's transgendered. I just want her to be happy," says Mom, sniffing.

She'll feel better when she finds the estrogen box. Perhaps I should leave the empty pouch on the top of my trash instead of hiding it in the wad of tissues. I want to be kind to her without opening the floodgates. I want her to be happy too. I back down the hallway all the way to my door, open and close it loudly, then tromp my way to the kitchen. I step into the light and stand there for a few seconds waiting for them to notice me, waiting for them to sense the change in me.

"There she is!" says Dad.

"Hey, Pumpkin," says Mom. "What's new with you? How's the homework going?"

Unfortunately, if she's not going to ask a quality question, she's going to have to suffer a little while longer.

Chapter Twenty-Three

That night, I find myself in a dream in Kansas's barn. It's dark and quiet and peaceful like it is in real life. I stroll down the alleyway and look in on all the horses. In real life, this is more difficult because the half doors are too tall for me to see over, so for the dream, I make all the doors stand open and the horses are contained in their stalls by nylon web stall guards. Kansas often uses stall guards in the daytime but she'd never leave the barn like this at night. Spike is examining his stall guard as though it's a problem to solve. He explores the clips that attach the guard to the wall with the end of his nose, then presses his face against the lowest strap, testing its strength.

"Don't you crawl under this," I warn him, scratching his neck.

The next stall is supposed to be Hambone's, but he's been replaced by the unicorn, unfortunately. He's lying in a mound of wood shavings when I arrive, but gets to his feet and stretches when he sees me. There's not enough light to tell if the horn is a still a twisted rainbow. I hope it's not. I'm embarrassed enough dreaming about a regular unicorn.

"What are you doing here?" I ask. I mean in my dream, but he doesn't take it that way.

"I'm catching up on my beauty rest," he says.

Shavings cling to his mane and tail. He gives himself a good shake and the air fills with a cloud of fine chips and fibers. Larger chunks remain stuck in the tangles of his mane. I conjure a curry comb into my hand and slip under the stall guard. "Let me help you with this," I say, lifting a section of mane in my hand.

"That would be helpful," says the unicorn. He lowers his head so I can reach the top of his neck.

He still has the bald spot halfway along his crest. I guess he's rubbed out the hairs. I wonder if this counts as trichotillomania and whether he is deeply unhappy too. If this dream is symbolizing the difficulties I am having in my relationship with Topaz, then perhaps I can use it as a practice session. I'm pondering what sort of quality question I could ask when I take a closer look and in the middle of the bald spot is a clear plastic patch identical to the one I have on my butt.

"Oh, come on!" I say. "What's this doing here?"

"I'm getting some unicorn hormone therapy," says the unicorn.

I've never heard of anything this ridiculous, but he looks serious, so it's probably best to humour him along. "Is it working?"

"Too soon to say."

I separate some knots in his mane with my fingers. He's going through the same process as me. Maybe he's not as ridiculous as I thought. "How will you know when it is working?"

"I'll be exactly like all the other unicorns, of course."

"But how will you know if you're feeling and thinking like all the other unicorns and you're not just feeling and thinking like a new mutant version of your self?"

"Well, that is the sixty-million dollar quality question, isn't it?"

I can tell from his tone that he's not going to discuss this any more and that he's going to make me answer my question myself. I finish brushing out all the shavings. Other than the missing section of mane, he's looking pretty good.

"How are things under the radar?" says the unicorn.

Something about his tone is annoying beyond words. "I'm not under the radar any more," I tell him. "I've joined the *Sistas.*"

"I suppose that's a start," says the unicorn, obviously not impressed. "But still... "

"But still what?" He is so frustrating.

"Your parents don't notice you have a genetic condition until you're fourteen. They don't notice that you've started taking estrogen... "

"It's only been a few hours," I say.

"You'd think they'd sense something. A unicorn parent would."

"I don't care. I don't want to be noticed, not for this. It's private."

"Some things you can't have both ways," says the unicorn.

I hate it when he's mysterious. Why doesn't he say what he means? I could punch him in the nose.

"Go ahead," he says. "Step up, why don't you. Take a stand. Take a swing. Come out of Neverland."

"Leave me alone," I say. I wiggle my toes until I wake up. He is such a jerk.

Chapter Twenty-Four

It's very early Sunday morning, and I'm lying in bed unable to sleep because I'm too busy feeling for signs of estrogen. I know I'm on a really low dose to begin with, but still, I should feel something.

I hear the phone going off in the kitchen; the answering machine cuts in after four rings. Usually, I can hear the muffled sounds of someone leaving a message, but not this time. It must have been a wrong number, because it's much too early for anyone to be phoning us, especially on a Sunday. Then the phone starts ringing again. It must be Grandpa—he's confused about the time zone difference between Saskatchewan and B.C. again. I throw off my quilt, do an Olympic dash to the kitchen and catch the phone on the third ring. Maybe my bone strength is improving, giving me superior athletic skills.

"Is that you, Pipsqueak?"

"Hi Grandpa. How are things in Saskatchewan?" I drop my voice to a whisper, "Or are you here again?" I check over my shoulder to make sure Mom or Dad hasn't followed me into the kitchen.

"What was that last bit?" says Grandpa.

His hearing is deteriorating—another problem of ageing. How do people stand it? "Never mind," I say with my normal voice. "How are you?"

"I'm great! I have good news. Our surprise is panning out well. All the paperwork cleared on Friday."

"Oh, that's wonderful." I feel so happy I could cry. Grandpa and Isobel are going to be living three blocks away!

"Are your Mom and Dad still in the dark?" says Grandpa.

"Yes, I haven't said a word." Do I tell him that I've hinted around the topic and they're nowhere close to ecstatic? He would be crushed.

"Great. We're flying out next weekend. Can you keep it a surprise until then? Isobel and I want to be there to see everyone's faces when they hear the news."

"I can keep a secret, Grandpa. But do you really think—"

"Can I speak to your mom, please, Pip? I need to reserve your guest room, if that's okay with her. And I thought she might want to have Sally and her brood over Saturday night for a big family get-together."

"It's seven in the morning, Grandpa. She's still in bed. She sleeps until nine on Sundays."

"Dang. Did I forget the time difference again? Oh well, we won't have to worry about that much longer, pretty soon we'll all be living in the same zone."

Same time zone maybe. But the same family zone? The same neighbourhood zone? The same social zone? I'm not sure how this is going to work at all.

"Can I give her the message, Grandpa?"

"How about you ask her to call me when she wakes up."

"Sure, I can do that."

"Isobel says hi, Pips."

"What about Isobel's family, Grandpa? When are you giving them the news?" I'm being vague about who Isobel's family is, because I can't bear to say Mr. Brumby's name out loud.

"Just a minute, Pips." I hang on while Grandpa has an indistinct conversation with Isobel at the other end. This goes on and on, and I turn to lean my back against the wall and suddenly become aware that I'm not alone in the kitchen.

"News about what?" says Mom, stretching her shoulders.

Think fast, Sylvia. "Grandpa and Isobel are coming out next weekend."

"Really? Give me that." Mom snatches the phone out of my hand. "Dad? It's me," she says. "Dad, are you there?"

"He's consulting with Isobel," I say.

"About what?"

I shrug as if I have no idea.

Mom taps her foot, waiting. Her attention wanders about the kitchen, but her back stiffens as soon as Grandpa comes back on the line. "She's telling who on Sunday?" she asks. "No, it's me, I'm up. Sylvia passed me the phone... Of course you can stay here, but what's this about news?... You have an announcement to make? That sounds exciting... "

Exciting like nuclear conflict.

"A family get-together is a great idea, which reminds me... "

Oh no, Mom, please.

"... we've been thinking it would be nice to have Isobel's relatives over, as a way of welcoming her into our family. Why don't we invite them to the party on Saturday?... How many would there be?... Just one?... Edward? And his last name is Brumby, right? And we've guessed he's Sylvia's math teacher?"

Edward Brumby. Mr. Brumby has a first name. Someone, somewhere, probably calls him Eddie. Oh ick.

"Do you want to give me his phone number?" says Mom. "Or I suppose I could ask Sylvie to pass him an invitation at school."

I shake my head hard enough that I'm surprised it doesn't fall off my neck. No invitation. No note. No Mr. Brumby. No No No.

"This will be wonderful," says Mom.

That's what she thinks.

This is going to be a disaster.

Mom continues to make plans with Grandpa, and I head to the family room aiming to hide on the computer for a while.

There's yet another message from Taylor with yet another link, which I click on completely by accident. I'm not in the mood for spiritual stuff, I just need some time out from family. The video loads with excruciating slowness. This is ridiculous. My finger poises to exit the site when the music starts along with a scene of white horses galloping through shallow water. The camera pulls back to show that the horses and the water are on a stage. How is this possible? A man rides a horse without saddle or bridle in the middle of an untethered herd. Another man directs a group of horses at liberty with invisible cues. And then there is a young woman, standing on the back of two horses, one slippered foot balanced on each bouncing rump. She holds a pair of reins in each hand, and the horses are cantering. How can she do this? It looks impossible. It looks like a dream.

Brooklyn wouldn't do any of these things for me.

Mom puts her hand on my shoulder and leans towards the screen. "That looks dangerous."

The music makes me want to cry. I say the only thing I can think of, "It's beautiful."

"You're not going to try that, are you Sylvie. That girl's not wearing a helmet or protective vest."

I am longing to do exactly what this girl is doing some day. Forget university, I am going to join this equestrian circus. But in the mean time, there is another clear opportunity. "You're right, Mom. I'll stick to eventing where there are a lot of safety protocols in place."

"You do that, Honey."

Mom pats my shoulder then twirls across the room while I bookmark the site and close the screen.

"I think they're getting married," she sings. "That's what the announcement is going to be."

"You don't know that for sure, Mom." She's already dancing at the wedding. I haven't seen her this happy in a long time. The disappointment is going to kill her.

"Well, what else could it be?" She stops mid-twirl. "You don't suppose there's something wrong, do you? If he's wanting to tell us that he's been diagnosed with cancer, he wouldn't label that an *announcement*, would he?"

"No, Mom. Of course not. Announcements are about good things."

"There you go then." She resumes dancing with an imaginary partner. "My father is re-marrying. I can buy a new dress. I should buy something new for the announcement party too, don't you think, Pumpkin?"

She is so happy. "Sure, Mom. Buy yourself something nice." That may help her feel better when everything falls apart.

Chapter Twenty-Five

I'm hosing Brooklyn's hock when Taylor wanders by. To be more accurate, Taylor is dragged by, at the end of Spike's lead rope. Spike is on the hunt for grass, and he knows the lushest growth is beside the manure pile, so that is where he's heading. He is permanently on a diet with the result that he always thinks he's starving. He could eat more if he was working, but he's not. He's a pet. Maximum exercise for him is a leisurely walk on the trails with Taylor.

"You shouldn't let him eat that grass," I yell across the yard to Taylor. "It's not good for him."

"He likes it," Taylor yells back. "And I like keeping him happy."

"Even if he gets metabolic syndrome and laminitis and has to be euthanized?" This is harsh. I'm not wrong, but I may have overstated my case.

Taylor turns her back to me. I don't expect she's going to answer. I concentrate on hosing Brooklyn's leg. We've been at it for ten minutes, so there's another five to go. Brooklyn is happy because he's eating from a pile of his regular hay. He's getting Spike's hay in his stall, but to keep his interest today I've found him a flake of blue-green hay that smells like summertime. He'll let me pour ice-cold water on his leg all day as long as he has this to eat. Taylor, for all her crazy ideas, was right to show me this bribery technique.

I hear Kansas's door close and look up to see her navigating the front stairs, Declan one step behind. Kansas is as big as a house. Her right arm curls around so her hand can support her middle back. Who would ever want to be pregnant?

"Hey," she says as she reaches me. "You're doing a good job."

Declan puts his arm around her shoulders. I think he's trying to hold her up.

"Thanks. Are you okay?"

She sighs wearily. "I didn't sleep much last night."

"World Cup of Soccer finals," says Declan, pointing to the beach ball.

She looks terrible. How can Declan joke about it?

"You could be napping right now," I say. "Everything's fine here, except for Taylor over-feeding Spike."

"I can't nap until my mom has cleaned up the *work site*. That's what she calls our house. I like the smell of sawdust. She says the baby will develop allergies if we bring her into that environment. She's been dusting and cleaning and vacuuming like a maniac all morning."

"She's a walking bundle of energy, that woman," says Declan.

"I've lost my home," says Kansas.

"Now, now," says Declan. "She's helping. Have a lie-down in the trailer why don't you? I have some horses to shoe." He tosses his truck key in the air and catches it with one hand.

"You're lucky—you can escape," says Kansas.

"I know it's hard for you, Stateside," says Declan. "But it would be good for you to let her help you."

Stateside? That's his nickname for her? Of course, she's not the kind of person who'd like being called *Pumpkin* or *Lovey-Dovey*. A laugh bursts out of me.

Kansas huffs with annoyance, then lurches free of Declan and plods to the travel trailer. She lets the door slam behind her.

"She's always thought she can do everything on her own," says Declan.

"It's good to be independent," I say in her defence.

"That it is," says Declan, "so far as it's possible."

"You don't mind Ida being here? My dad doesn't like in-laws. He says they're incomprehensible."

Declan considers me thoughtfully. "Ida is an essential part of Kansas's life, whether they get along well or not, and Kansas is the most precious thing in my life." He shrugs as though he's made everything perfectly clear. "Now I'm off to work." He's in his truck and out the driveway before I can articulate half a question.

I don't understand what Declan meant. I can think of all sorts of exceptions, like how Franco is part of Logan's life, but that doesn't mean they help each other. Families are very confusing.

Across the yard stands Taylor, who is, without doubt, essential to my life. I shut off the hose and lead Brooklyn to join Spike in the long grass.

"I hardly think that hand-grazing for a few minutes is going to catapult him into metabolic syndrome, if you were serious about that comment," says Taylor.

"You're right, it won't." All my spite has somehow evaporated.

Taylor says thank you, but squints at me suspiciously.

"I watched the video you sent me this morning," I say.

"It was fantastic. I can't believe what those people did with their horses."

"Wasn't it amazing?" says Taylor. "And they were all so happy."

"It's made me think there could be more to horses for me than riding cross-country courses," I say.

"Funny," says Taylor. "It's made me think Spike wouldn't mind if I rode him."

"You could let him eat more food if he had more exercise."

Taylor laughs. "Well, he'd like that for sure."

The air around us becomes warm and soft. When I draw it into my lungs, my body warms and softens. I feel how wonderful and kind and gentle Taylor is, as if her aura of goodness extends around both of us. Plus we now have a meeting of minds and a new project to do together. We can watch videos, and learn, and practice with our horses.

Taylor peers at me. "There's something different about you," she says.

She can tell! Somebody finally noticed! "I started the estrogen. I haven't told anyone else."

"Oh, Sylvia!" Taylor bounces on her toes. "Oh, this is so exciting!" She grabs me by the shoulders and pulls me snug against her body. It's nice that she's happy again, but I wish she wasn't so dramatic, making loud squeally noises as she squashes my face into her bra. I pull away as soon as I can. Brooklyn has stepped back to the end of the lead rope and is eyeing us cautiously, on guard for another eruption. Nothing ever surprises Spike, whose nose stays stuffed in the grass.

"You won't be able to tell for a while," I say, placing my hands lightly on my flat chest and fluttering my fingers.

"I know that," says Taylor. "Can you feel anything yet? Anywhere?"

I shake my head. "I put on the first patch last night, and it's a very low dose. They say it'll be weeks before there's... " I can't say it.

"Spotting?" says Taylor enthusiastically.

Oh, I really wish she wouldn't. Why do people have to put words on all this personal stuff? I know she means well, but surely, some things are better left unsaid.

"Let me know when you start, and we can go to the pharmacy and I can help you pick out the best—"

"No!" Here comes the talk about feminine hygiene products. I don't want to hear it. "I mean, thank you. But my mom has already—"

"Your mom is stuck in the dark ages. I have sisters. We know everything there is to know about—"

"Okay, whatever, I promise I'll tell you, then we can go shopping," I say, though there's no way this will happen. I intend to do research online, anonymously, privately, and sneak off to Pharmasave on a Sunday morning when everybody's still asleep.

Taylor doesn't believe me. Her suspicious look returns. "You are a peculiar soul," she says, eyeing me closely. "But I love you. And I'm sorry about giving you a bad time about galloping Brooklyn and making you defensive. I see what you were getting at, with that crack about metabolic syndrome. You're a sly one, Sylvia. You were doing the same thing to me as I did to you, forcing me to question whether letting my horse do what he wants and be happy in the short term is good for him in the long run."

What? Sly? Me? "I'm glad you caught that," I say.

"Maybe the estrogen is working already!" says Taylor.

Maybe it is.

Chapter Twenty-Six

Monday morning, Mom is in a complete flutter about preparing a hand-written invitation for Mr. Brumby; I am to deliver it to him at school. She says this personal touch is much nicer than a phone call.

"I can't find any invitation cards," she says, digging through the desk drawers in the family room. "I'll have to buy one on my lunch hour, and write it tonight."

Dad tells her not to be ridiculous. He says we have plenty of free cards made by the Foot and Mouth Painting Artists, and from the Wildlife Federation. Mom spends half an hour deciding which card would be suitable. In my opinion, none of them are. It would have been better and quicker to go to the mall and buy a new one that is more appropriate than one with a monarch butterfly perched on a puny mauve flower.

Mom reads aloud to me when she's finished writing. *"Dear Mr. Brumby, We're hoping that you can join us for dinner at a family gathering this Saturday (6 p.m.) as we welcome your mother, Isobel, and Henry (our father/grandfather) who are visiting from Saskatchewan. With warm regards from Evelyn and Tony Forrester, and of course Sylvie.*" She looks up, obviously pleased. "Is that good enough? Should I say he can bring a date?"

"No, that's good enough, Mom."

Mom stuffs the card in a coordinated mauve envelope and writes Mr. Brumby's name on the outside.

"Do you really think it's okay like this, or would it be more friendly to address him as *Edward?*"

"No, that's good the way it is," I say. Edward. I'll never get used to this. I will never be able to call him Edward. Or Uncle Edward.

Mom tucks in the flap of the envelope and passes it to me. It smells sweetly of her hand cream. "Put it in your backpack, Honey. And make sure he gets it today, so he has time to plan. We want to be sure he can make it to the party."

Right. Let's make this into a disaster in every possible way.

Mom taps me on my arm. "I know he's not your favourite, Pumpkin, but I've told Isobel we're inviting him. You will give him the note, won't you?"

"Of course," I say, but only because there's no way out. If I forget to deliver it, sooner or later my mom will find out. There's no sense in upsetting her, or Isobel for that matter. I'll have to be mature and do the difficult right thing.

My backpack is in the garage, ready for me beside my bike. I drop the envelope on the cement floor while I open my pack. The zipper sticks and I have to toss the pack on the workbench to sort it out. It lands beside a bottle of fish fertilizer, which isn't supposed to be there—stinky things like this are meant to be stored in the garden shed.

The bottle is old, the cap is cracked and oozing, and there's a small, yellowish puddle accumulating around the base. Fortunately my backpack has landed clear of it.

With much effort, I manage to release the zipper, then look around for the envelope and find it under my foot. I pick it up and brush off my tread mark, or most of it. I consider the yellow puddle, and how less inviting that would smell than the scent of my mom's hand cream. I wonder if Mr. Brumby might possibly take a big fat hint and decline the invitation. What did the unicorn tell me? Take a swing. Take a stand. I can do that.

There's no one waiting for me at my locker at school. No tormentors and no supporter either. I am able to hang up my jacket and organize my books in peace for a change. I tuck the envelope inside my math textbook and head off to class. The fish smell is so subtle that I hardly notice it. My plan is to hand it to Mr. Brumby after class, when everyone else has left.

I'm the last one to take my seat. Topaz is slumped ahead of me, her head on her desk, the bald spot visible for the entire world to see, and larger than ever. Logan is behind me. When I take my seat, he says hello politely, which is very troubling. Topaz is singing softly to herself. Logan is making clicking sounds with his tongue. How am I supposed to be able to concentrate on math when I am surrounded by drama?

Mr. Brumby is late. Maybe he's sick and we'll have a substitute. My heart leaps. Maybe he'll be sick all week and won't be able to come to the party. The seconds tick by and the class becomes more restless. Topaz pulls a hair out of her head and inspects the follicle.

Logan says, "What's that smell? Did something die?"

"Did you fart again, Losino?" says Graham from the seat behind him.

"It's not me," says Logan. He leans forward, sniffing the air. He could so easily say that the smell was coming from me. I have treated him badly; I have hurt him. I catch his eyes, his lovely chocolate eyes, and I melt as I have never done before. What is this helpless feeling? It's as though my insides have all turned to goo. "I'm sorry," I whisper.

"Losino fart alert!" shouts Graham. All the boys laugh and all the girls groan, except for Topaz, who is still off in her own world.

Logan stands up and uses his hands to fan the air in Graham's direction.

The door at the front of the room clicks open. "Detention for Logan Losino," says Mr. Brumby. "Anyone else care to join him?" He looks terrible. His eyes are rimmed with pink and his hair looks as bad as Topaz's. He has a box of tissues tucked under one arm.

The room falls silent.

I raise my hand.

"Yes, Sylvia?"

I stand up. "I would like to join him," I say. "He wasn't the only one goofing off."

"That was a rhetorical question," says Mr. Brumby.

A chair grates on the floor behind us. I turn to see Graham on his feet. "I'd like to join Logan too," he says.

In seconds, ten more people are standing. I poke Topaz, who looks around, bewildered. "Is there a fire drill?" she asks.

"Get up," I whisper.

Then everyone is on their feet.

Mr. Brumby is purple. What can he do? He can't send us all to the principal's office for requesting detentions.

"Sit down," he says. "Open your books, and complete the exercises in chapter eleven. Not a sound from any of you;

I will be right outside." And he leaves. I'm sure he would have slammed the door if it wasn't on a pneumatic hinge.

We all take our seats. I open my textbook. The scent of fish wafts anew, but no one says anything. Logan pokes me with a finger, which must mean something, but I don't know what.

I make sure I'm the last one to leave at the end of class. Mr. Brumby has not reappeared. I place the invitation in the centre of his desk and stare at it. I feel like I'm kicking Mr. Brumby while he's down. There's a smear of dirt across the envelope, and the stink of the fish fertilizer is a lot stronger than I intended. The invitation looks and smells like garbage, and that's where it belongs. I pick it up, rip it into quarters and drop it in the trash. I'll deal with my mom later.

Logan is in the hallway, bent over, tying his shoe. He takes a long time getting it right. When he sees me he gives his shoe one final pat and stands up. Has he been waiting for me? Maybe he wants to tell me how much I stink.

"Thanks for supporting me," he says.

"It was the right thing to do," I say. "Any sign of Mr. Brumby?"

Logan shakes his head. "I can't believe how brave you were. You really started something in there. I think I owe you an apology for whatever it was that I said on Saturday."

"You thought there was something weird going on with Mr. Brumby, and you thought I'd changed," I remind him. I take a deep breath and let it go. All I need to add now, to fix everything, is: *You were right about both. Mr. Brumby is going to be my uncle, and I am being transformed by estrogen.* I take another breath. If I tell him, he will start scrutinizing all my interactions with Mr. Brumby. And my chest.

"Sylvia, I said that because I was upset. Even if you change, you'll still be you."

He is so nice and kind and understanding... and crazy. "That doesn't make sense," I say. "If I change, how can I still be me?"

Logan shrugs and laughs. "Who else could you be?" He gives me the soppy look. I still don't know how to react to it. Part of me wants to hug him and part of me wants to slap his face.

Fortunately the bell sounds and we have sixty seconds to make it to our next class. Logan touches my arm. "We're still friends then?"

"Yeah. Sure."

The relief that washes across his face slays me. I have to look away. I clutch my books to my chest, and we join the stream of students rushing to class.

Chapter Twenty-Seven

When I arrive at the stable after school, all is eerily quiet. Taylor never comes on Mondays because she has a regular babysitting gig. Neither Declan's nor Kansas's trucks are in the yard.

I find Ida, Kansas's mom, asleep in the tack room. Beside her are a bucket of water, a sponge, a bar of saddle soap and a tin of leather conditioner. Kansas's double bridle is in pieces on several sheets of newspaper spread at her feet. I wouldn't dare take apart a double bridle—I'd never be able to put all the parts back together properly. Ida is sitting slumped in a chair, her chin on her chest, making whistling noises through her nose.

I try to back away without disturbing her, but my foot accidentally taps a metal bucket, which clanks on the cement floor and she jerks awake.

"Oh Sylvia," she says, putting a hand to her chest, "you frightened me. I was waiting for the leather to dry. I must have fallen asleep."

"I'm sorry I woke you," I say.

"Oh, it's nothing, I can fall asleep at the drop of a hat during the day. Nights are a different matter, unfortunately." She coats a rag with some leather conditioner, selects the brow band from the tangle at her feet and sets to rubbing in the oil. Her knuckles are huge, and one thumb shoots off at an odd angle. "Are you riding Brooklyn today? He is such a fine horse."

"No, he's still on stall rest. I can't ride him before Thursday."

Ida nods. "You're letting him heal naturally. I think that's a good idea. Do you need any help with him? Kansas is at the doctor's for what she hopes is one last checkup."

"No, I don't need any help, thanks." Ida has all the physical substance of a bird. I can't imagine her helping with Brooklyn. But then I wouldn't have expected her to be a maniac with a vacuum cleaner either.

"I understand you're taking a babysitting course so you can help Kansas with the baby. That's very kind of you. I won't worry as much about her when I'm gone, knowing the support she has here."

"You're not staying? I thought you were all moved into the trailer."

She places the brow band on a dry section of newspaper and picks up a cheek piece. On a regular bridle there are two cheek pieces; a double bridle has four. Ida doesn't seem at all worried about what will be going where. "Oh no, this is just temporary. They want to be on their own. I won't stay for long, unless there are problems with the baby—not that I'll be a great deal of help there. My maternal instincts have always skewed more in the direction of puppies, kittens and ponies. But I can help out with other things."

I upturn the bucket and take a seat on it so I can better

digest this surprising confession. "But you had Kansas when she was a baby."

"Oh, sure," says Ida. "And she was lovely. But I was never one of those women who went nuts about babies, wanting to hold them and smell the tops of their heads at any opportunity."

"I thought all women loved babies. Normal women, I mean."

Ida shakes her head. "Not me. I guess I'm not normal." She laughs, as though this is perfectly okay.

"I like puppies, kittens and ponies too," I tell her.

She doesn't even look up. "I thought as much."

I wait for her to say something about my probably not being able to have babies anyway, given my Turner Syndrome, which she must know all about by now. I wait for her to turn this into a big, meaningful, teaching-moment conversation, but she doesn't. She finishes polishing the cheek piece and picks up another. Her skin is pale, and there are dark hairs sprouting from her upper lip. I try to imagine what she looked like when she was my age. I try to erase the wrinkles and make her hair dark brown and shiny like Kansas's, but I can't.

"Did you ride before, when you were younger?" I ask her.

"Oh, yes. I loved riding. I rode as long as I could, but then the arthritis got me."

"But you can still do things. You can clean tack, you can vacuum, why can't you ride?"

She stops polishing, and her hands drop into her lap. "Well, I suppose I got tired of the pain, and the work, and the expense, and the responsibility. The divorce didn't help. But horses are large unpredictable animals—they're risky to be around for people who have lost strength and flexibility. I know it's difficult for someone at your end of life to understand."

"You're right," I say. "I'd die if I had to quit riding."

"That's what I thought too, when I was your age. Life changes. You adapt."

I can't imagine adapting to not riding. A week of stall rest has been as much as I can tolerate. "Not me. I'm going to ride horses until I'm ninety. It's all I want to do."

"Well, good luck with that," says Ida. "And for goodness sake, don't dwell on it. Enjoy yourself. I'm sure you're more adaptable than you think. We all have to be, when it comes to ageing. We have to be able to move on."

"My grandpa is moving from Saskatchewan into a seniors retirement village three blocks from our house," I say.

"How nice for everyone. You must all be very pleased," says Ida. She drops the cheek piece and picks up a pair of reins, the thin ones that attach to the curb bit. "Three blocks," she says ambiguously.

"I'm pleased, but I'm the only one who knows. My parents are concerned about his independence and their privacy. I think they'd prefer he move to Victoria."

"They'll work it out," says Ida. "Families may fall apart at times, but usually they fall back together again. Kansas and I have not always gotten along, you know."

I fake a surprised expression.

"Right," says Ida. "Go enjoy your horse, Sylvia."

Brooklyn is waiting for me in his small rehab paddock. He's happy to see me because he's finished his hay and has nothing to do. I take him and a flake of Spike hay to the wash rack, and hose down his leg while he nibbles away. I think about what Ida said for a few minutes but then my attention is taken by the interesting patterns of pink and grey skin that emerge on Brooklyn's leg as the water saturates his coat. When he was young, his coat would have been dark all over, except for white stockings. Now he's white everywhere, and he's not even very old.

After twenty minutes have passed, I return Brooklyn to his paddock. I stop at the tack room before I head home, because I want to tell Ida that she can ride Brooklyn when he's sound again, if she likes. He is small, and most of the time he's predictable, and it won't cost her anything. But Ida has gone. The newspapers have been picked up and the conditioner and saddle soap are back on the shelf. Kansas's double bridle is hanging, fully assembled, on its holder as it always does, except for being cleaner and shinier than I've ever seen it.

Chapter Twenty-Eight

Dad has cooked steaks on the barbecue and Mom has made a huge green salad with dried cranberries and slivered almonds. I'm on my second helping of salad. Mom and Dad have been busy telling each other about their day and I haven't been listening. I've been thinking about Saturday, and whether Ida is right about families, or whether sometimes they break and never grow back together.

Out of the blue, Mom turns to me and asks if I gave Mr. Brumby the invitation.

"It wasn't a good day," I say. "I think the timing wasn't right."

"Timing?" says Mom.

"Something happened. Mr. Brumby gave Logan Losino a detention and asked if anyone wanted to join him, and I said I did, and then everyone else said they did too."

"A revolution," says Dad. "The bastard finally got what he had coming."

"Tony, really," says Mom.

"That's not what it felt like, Dad. It was more like an uprising. We rose up. I wasn't even angry."

"That sounds wonderful, Honey," says Mom. "I think you've matured. That was a very adult thing to do. You're turning into a lovely young woman."

Okay, obviously she has found the open box of estrogen patches with one packet missing. Please let's not turn this into a big thing. "Mom—"

"Still sounds like a rebellion to me," says Dad.

Mom sighs. Fortunately and unfortunately for me, Dad has broken her focus. "Well, I told Isobel we were going to invite him. I suppose I'll give him a phone call after dinner."

Oh, I wish she wouldn't. He already thinks I'm a troublemaker after catching me fighting with Topaz in the hall, and if he now thinks I've instigated a rebellion, he'll hate me even more. I don't want him at the party. It's going to be bad enough as it is, with Grandpa's secret being revealed.

"Mom—"

"Tell him to bring a date," says Dad. "Some tough roller derby chick who can keep him in line."

"For heaven's sake Tony, you're not making this any easier," says Mom.

"Sure I am, where's your sense of humour? Besides, I can handle the guy if he steps out of line. I deal with difficult people at work all the time—there's a lot of tension over money issues."

"You don't say," says Mom.

I try to remember what I did in math class. Rising up was wonderful then; why can't I do it now?

I'm loading dishes in the dishwasher when Mom gets Mr. Brumby on the phone. I'd prefer not to hear this conversation, so I make a lot of extra noise dropping the cutlery into the holders. Finally, Mom covers the mouthpiece with her hand and tells me to hush, so I have to be satisfied with humming to myself and running water in the sink. What if he tells her I was caught fighting in the hall? What if he says I was almost expelled, and that I instigated a riot in the classroom today? What if he loses his temper with my mom and screams at her that he doesn't want to come to her stupid party?

Mom finishes the call and comes over and turns off the tap. "That went well," she says. "He sounded perfectly reasonable and delighted to come on Saturday, as long as he's over his cold."

He must be saving up all that information for a more devastating time to tell everyone. He won't forget. I wonder if I'll be eligible for foster care after my parents disown me.

Chapter Twenty-Nine

On Thursday Brooklyn (and I) are released from stall rest. I walk him around the ring under the joint supervision of Kansas and Ida.

"I think he's still short on the left hind," says Kansas.

"I don't see it," says Ida. "Look how even he is in the hips. Ask for a little trot, Sylvia."

Kansas waves her hand and starts to object, so I quickly ask Brooklyn to trot before she can get a word out.

"There," says Ida. "See? He's regular as a metronome."

"I guess," says Kansas.

"He's fine?" I say. I am on cloud nine.

"You take it easy with him for a few days," says Kansas. "Gentle walk and trot only. You can't canter before Saturday."

"That's fine," I say. I'm riding. That's enough.

Kansas puts a hand to her tummy and looks thoughtful.

"Another one?" says Ida.

Kansas nods.

"I think I'll call Declan," says Ida.

Kansas nods again. There's no fight left in her. Or she's saving it for something else.

My baby sister is coming.

Without a glance in my direction, Kansas and Ida make their way back to the house, the big hippopotamus leaning on the tiny bird. In about five minutes, Declan's truck roars down the driveway at a hundred kilometres an hour and he too disappears into the house. I ride Brooklyn for another ten minutes, then put him back in his paddock.

My baby sister is coming.

I find Taylor in Spike's stall, her arms around his neck, her cheek pressed against his ear. "Wait a minute," she tells me. "We're communicating."

I watch as Spike's great long ears flop from one direction to another. To me, he looks like he's sleeping.

"He says he wouldn't mind my riding him if that meant we could explore farther from the barn," says Taylor.

Oh boy. As if that needed psychic communication. "That's good to hear," I say.

She unwraps her arms and stands there, leaning on his shoulder.

"He'd like to spend more time with Brooklyn. He can't stand Hambone. He says Brooklyn has had enough of being constantly bossed around by Hambone too and has enjoyed being in a private paddock for the last week."

"Even though he was confined in a smaller space?" I say doubtfully.

Taylor shrugs. "Apparently. And by the way, Spike says Brooklyn is fine now. There's no more pain in his leg."

"Really? Oh that's great!" I don't care if this is information from the psychic realm. It's good to confirm what Ida saw.

"He said you knew that already. He said that Brooklyn communicates with you and that you listen to him all the time."

Whoa. I nod as if in agreement.

Taylor says, "You didn't know that, did you."

"I don't know. I did and I didn't. But it's nice."

Taylor smiles. "It's wonderful to watch you changing," she says. "My mom's really pleased too."

"You told your mom? About my estrogen patch?"

Taylor pales. "It was private? I forgot. It was such good news, that's all."

"She'll tell everyone. You know what she's like. I'll be the centre of attention on Saturday, which I hate. Everyone's going to be staring at my chest. It's bad enough that my mom has figured it out."

"Sylvia, I'm sorry."

"And Mr. Brumby's going to be there, and Grandpa's going to make his big announcement, and it is not going to be what everyone expects and everything is going to be a huge mess."

"Oh my," says Taylor. She glances behind her. "Spike says you need to chill."

"You are full of shit," I say. I turn to leave them there, communing, but at the last second I add, "And Kansas is having her baby." And then I storm home.

Chapter Thirty

My bad luck continues after I'm home. When I change out of my riding breeches, I notice a lump in my underwear. Somehow my patch has been rubbed out of place, even though I hardly rode for any time at all. All week I've been taking the briefest of showers and being careful with my towel to ensure the patch stayed on, and now it's off anyway. I stick it back but during dinner I feel it bunching up between my cheek and the chair and it's all I can do to pretend there's nothing wrong. I leave it until later.

By eight o'clock there is still no word from Kansas. I don't know if she went to the hospital or not. I decide to relax by taking a soothing bath. I ball up the patch in a wodge of toilet paper and toss it in the trash. Then I climb in the tub for a well-deserved soak.

Mom and Dad are making up the guest bedroom down the hall. They're both laughing and having a good time. Mom loves weddings and parties. She was desperate to decorate the guest room in a wedding motif. Fortunately she has a lot of other preparations to do before the family event on Saturday, and Dad was able to talk her out of it.

They're a pretty good team when they have a project. On Saturday, Dad will be barbecuing burgers and he has already bought a fresh propane tank, mowed the back lawn and cleaned all our patio furniture. When I put my bike away earlier, I found four bottles of champagne tucked into a corner of the garage. I wonder if they'll be popped after the real announcement happens, which has nothing to do with a wedding. What do people drink when they hear bad news?

Mom has a grocery list for Saturday that grows an inch every time I look at it, even though she insists she's keeping everything simple. There's a cake to pick up from the bakery, and fixings for salads, and fruit juice, and paper plates, and buns. I added *Emergency First Aid Kit*, but when Mom saw this she looked at me funny and erased it.

I examine my torso as I lie in the tub. There's been no visible change. I raise an arm and a leg and watch the water run off. Perhaps my bones look healthier.

After my bath, back in my bedroom, I find the box of patches in my dresser drawer. The sock has been moved from the top, so if I didn't know before, I know now that Mom has been in snooping. No surprise there. I pull out a fresh pouch and put the box back without any tricks. It doesn't matter any more if Mom snoops or not.

I carefully select a new spot on my buttock and apply patch number two.

I wish Kansas would phone. Or Declan. Or Ida.

But no one does.

That night I dream I'm at the stable. There are no lights on in the house. All is quiet. The two trucks are parked in the yard. The horses are munching hay in their stalls. There is no sign of the unicorn.

I fall into a restless sleep and have no more dreams before the morning. I awake feeling tired and ill-prepared to face the day.

It doesn't help that the first thing Mom tells me when I arrive in the kitchen is that I can't go to the barn after school because Grandpa and Isobel are arriving on the two o'clock flight and she needs me at home to welcome them.

"Can't you leave a key for them under the mat?" I say.

"Sorry, Pumpkin. They're coming all the way from Saskatchewan. I want someone here when they arrive. It's good manners. Neither your father nor I can leave work early today."

"They'll probably have a present for you from their trip to Reno," says Dad.

Yeah, right.

"It's only one day," says Mom. "Well, two days to be more exact. You won't be able to go Saturday either. There'll be too much to do here, and you have to attend your babysitting course in the afternoon. That will be difficult enough."

"But I was going to start cantering again on Saturday," I say. I am crestfallen. "And Kansas—"

"Sorry, Honey. Family has to take precedence here. And your commitment to your class."

"What about my commitment to Brooklyn? Does that not count for anything?" It's inconceivable that I not visit the barn until Sunday.

But my parents are together on this one. There's no budging either of them. They give each other a big smooch before heading out the door to work. I'm left there, alone, sitting on my patch, defeated already. Probably this bad start is a sign of how the rest of the day will unfold. Mr. Brumby has been away since Monday and we've had a substitute teacher who is young and happy and knows nothing about math, so we've been discussing climate change and current events. How long can a cold last? Mr. Brumby is going to be furious when he eventually comes back, because we'll be so far behind in his curriculum. Especially me. Even when I'm caught up I'm still behind, if that makes any sense. Plus, Mr. Brumby is going to be upset with me because of the revolution I started. I can't face him, not today.

I wish I could have a cold.

As a matter of fact, my throat is feeling kind of sore.

I sniff through my nose. Stuffy. I grab a tissue and dab at a nostril. I cough.

How fast can a cold come on? Would my mom believe this?

It's worth a try. I shuffle back to my room, climb into bed, pull the covers over my head and fall back to sleep.

I'm awakened by the doorbell at noon.

Grandpa and Isobel are waiting on the steps, their rental car behind them on the driveway.

"Surprise!" says Grandpa. "We caught an earlier flight... hey, Pips, what are you doing here? Why aren't you at school?"

I rub my eyes. "I stayed home. I had a cold, and I was really tired. Or I thought I had a cold." I take a deep breath through my unclogged nostrils. "I'm fine now." How did that happen?

"Sylvia, it's wonderful to see you," says Isobel, giving me a big hug. "And it's so warm here! It was minus twenty when we left home. I'm going to need to change my clothes."

"I'll get lunch," I say as they wheel their luggage to the guestroom.

I make peanut butter and banana sandwiches, set the

table and put on the kettle, because I know that Isobel enjoys her tea.

She hugs me again when she finds me in the kitchen.

"I brought you a present," she says.

"My dad said you might bring me something from Reno."

Isobel laughs. "We can tell him that if you like." She hands me a crumpled package. "The wrapping didn't travel well."

I tear it off. There's a blue t-shirt inside.

"It's partly a token of our appreciation for keeping our secret safe," says Isobel. "But mostly it's something that I thought might be useful for you sometimes."

From most people, this means a t-shirt with a tacky painting of a horse in fluorescent, unnatural colours, but I can see this isn't the case as I pick up the shoulders. There's a large red heart in the middle of the shirt, and on either side, in white block capitals, is the letter *I*.

"*I Heart I?*" I say.

Isobel nods. "Lovely, isn't it?"

I run my fingers across the shirt. I could wear this to math class and be safe from the onslaughts of Mr. Brumby. I could wear it in the hallway and flash it at Amber. I could wear it at dinner when my parents are arguing. I could wear it tomorrow for the family get-together. I could wear it all the time. It would be just like wearing my eventing protective vest, but for a whole other range of hazards.

"Where's my lunch?" asks Grandpa. "Let's eat up then we'll drive over and have a look at the new hacienda."

"Let's walk, Henry. I'd like to stretch my legs after that flight. It's certainly close enough."

"You're right, Isobel," says Grandpa, taking a seat at the table. "We're going to be virtually next door. We'll be able to drop by for peanut butter sandwiches whenever we want." He takes a bite. "This is delicious, Pipsqueak. You'll make a great chef when you grow up."

Isobel and I sit down, and Isobel tucks into her lunch. "Sylvia, this is the best peanut butter and banana sandwich I've ever had."

"Surely not better than the one I made you, Mrs. Brumby," says Grandpa.

I almost need the Heimlich maneuver. I'd just swallowed a mouthful, and hearing the Brumby name makes my throat muscles go into spasm. I take a drink of water to wash it down.

Mr. Brumby will be in my house tomorrow. He'll try to flirt with Auntie Sally, but she won't have anything to do with him because she'll be too busy announcing that I am taking estrogen and everyone will stare at my chest. Mr. Brumby will have an argument about numbers with my dad, who won't back down, and Mr. Brumby will punch him in the nose. After they get back from the hospital emergency department, my parents will find out that Isobel and Grandpa will be living three blocks away, close enough to lose their independence and constantly infringe on our privacy. Dad will have wasted a lot of money on champagne that will not be opened because there is not going to be a wedding. Isobel will be so embarrassed by her son's behaviour that she will fly back to Saskatchewan.

I drink some more water.

Isobel says, "Do you want to model that t-shirt for me, Sylvia? They only had mediums, so it will probably slip right over what you're wearing."

I pick up the shirt from where I'd left it on the seat of the extra chair. I slide into it and stand up. The hem comes halfway to my knees.

"You could wear it as a night shirt," says Isobel.

Yes, I could use it to fend off that annoying unicorn. I stroke the red heart smooth across my stomach. I can feel it working.

"I can wear it whenever I want," I say.

I Heart I.

Chapter Thirty-One

Saturday morning after breakfast Grandpa asks me how I'm doing with Brooklyn.

"We're doing great," I say. "He was on stall rest for a week but he's fine now and I was going to start cantering again today but—"

"Well we'd like to be there to see that, wouldn't we Isobel?" says Grandpa.

Mom says, "Sylvia doesn't have time to spend at the stable today. There's too much to do preparing for tonight, and she has her babysitting course this afternoon."

"Oh, that's too bad," says Isobel.

"Nonsense!" says Grandpa. "We'll drive her to the barn and have her back here by lunchtime."

Dad sips his coffee and doesn't say anything out loud, but I figure he's thinking about the *interfering old goat* problem again. He looks at my mom and offers her a knowing smile.

"Oh whatever," says Mom. "I don't have time to argue

with you, I have a haircut at ten, and then I have to finish off the shopping and make all the salads."

"I can help with that this afternoon," says Isobel.

"Oh, I don't think so. You're the honoured guest."

Isobel looks puzzled. She's always helped out in the past. I know what's going on. Mom is so focused on the potential wedding that she already sees Isobel as the bride who mustn't lift a finger on her big day. Mom is way out ahead of herself. When she eventually hears the real announcement, she's going to wish she'd saved herself all the trouble and ordered pizzas.

"I thought we'd take a drive this afternoon," says Grandpa. I know what's going on here too. Grandpa wants to decorate the new condominium with balloons and streamers and take everyone over there after he makes the announcement at the party.

Isobel looks from my mom to my grandpa and back again. She can help prevent my mom from having a nervous breakdown overworking in the kitchen, or she can help prevent my grandpa from having a heart attack blowing up too many balloons.

Tough choice.

Grandpa wins. "A drive would be nice, Henry," she says.

Dad says, "I can toss a salad, Ev."

I grab the opportunity and leap from my chair. "I'll change into my riding clothes. I'll be ready in two minutes."

The stable is deserted, except for the horses, of course, which means it's not deserted at all, but there are no humans around. It's too early for Taylor, who never makes it to the barn before eleven on the weekends. Kansas's truck is there, but Declan's is gone.

Hambone and his herd are out in the pasture, heads down, eating grass and looking content, or as content as is possible with Hambone menacingly in charge. Usually, Kansas brings them in at night and lets them out again in the morning. I wonder if they spent the whole night outside. Maybe Kansas has been in hospital since Thursday and no one told me. Maybe the baby died, and no one wanted to tell me that either.

Brooklyn is in his paddock picking up the last few pieces of hay. Obviously he's been fed his breakfast, but his stall hasn't been mucked out to Kansas's standards.

"Where is everybody?" says Grandpa. "It's like a ghost town."

"I think Kansas is having her baby. I haven't seen her since Thursday, and she was having twinges then." If anything's gone wrong, I'll feel terrible for wanting to have a Turner Syndrome sister. I wipe my sweating palms on my breeches.

"Sometimes these things take a while," says Isobel. "There can be false starts, especially for the first one. I'm sure we would have heard if there was any news. Why don't you tack up your horse and show us how he's doing?"

Grandpa and Isobel take a seat on the bench beside the riding arena. They are still sitting there, holding hands and chatting, when Brooklyn and I emerge from the barn five minutes later. I lead him to the mounting block and climb on, though my heart isn't in it. I can't stop thinking about Kansas.

"Which leg did he injure?" says Grandpa.

"The left hind."

"And what was the rehab plan?"

"Stall rest and cold hosing for a week, then gradually return to work. I walked and trotted for fifteen minutes on Thursday."

Grandpa checks his watch. "I'll time you, Pipsqueak. How about ten minutes of walk, five of trot, and two of lope or canter or whatever you call it."

"I'll take some pictures," says Isobel, struggling in her purse for a camera. "Where's the best place to stand, Sylvia?"

And just like that, I'm all absorbed in riding and taking care of Brooklyn, and feeling for the evenness of his stride, and finding good angles for Isobel to take photos. Brooklyn is happy when I finally ask for canter, and I think he'd like to go really fast but I make him listen to me, and we canter around the ring and don't do any circles because that would place more strain on his hock, though Brooklyn doesn't know that, of course. I know, and I'm responsible for him, so we do it my way.

Chapter Thirty-Two

After lunch, I ride my bike to the recreation centre. I'm there before Topaz, who arrives five minutes late, looking even more dishevelled than usual. I'm no fashion expert, but even to me, it's obvious that her pants and shirt clash. Her hair hasn't been washed for a few days, or combed for that matter.

I don't have time to dwell on Topaz, however, because class is great. Finally, we learn about baby CPR and what to do if a baby chokes. We practice on a special doll. It's scary and fantastic at the same time. We practice dialing 911 too, which seems ridiculous to me, but the instructor says people who panic forget how to do the simplest things, and that practice is the best way to prepare for anything.

I wish I could prepare for everything. If only I had a plan that I could practice for all the awful things that might happen, like Mr. Brumby having a volcanic eruption in my living room, or my parents disowning my grandparents.

When class ends, I strap on my bike helmet and follow

Topaz down the hall to the lobby. She stops when she nears the main windows, and slides to hide behind a pillar. Outside the door, Franco's car is idling by the curb. Franco is in the driver's seat. There's no sign of Amber. This is very odd.

"Franco's here to pick you up? Why isn't Amber with him?"

Topaz has a hunk of hair in her fingers. Her eyes are full of tears. "My parents took her wilderness camping. I had to stay home for this stupid course. Franco's here for me. He says he prefers me over Amber, but he can't tell her yet."

"You're kidding." That probably wasn't the right thing to say, but Topaz doesn't take offence.

"I know," she says. "I try avoiding him, I try making myself look a unattractive, but nothing puts him off." She wipes her eyes on her sleeve.

"You've been looking like this on purpose? Because of Franco?"

She nods. "And if he doesn't break up with her, he wants a threesome. It's always been his dream, he says, with twins."

"But you're not even identical."

"I know that."

This is when a plan would come in handy. But how could I have predicted an event like this? I say the first thing that comes into my mind. "Let me help you. I'll get my bike and meet you at the back door and we'll sneak out of here together."

Topaz shakes her head. "Where would I go? He'll find me. It's my fault anyway. I flirted with him, only to show Amber I could. But he took me seriously, and now he has the perfect opportunity."

"Come to my house. My mom will know what to do." Good grief, the unexpected things that come out of my mouth. "We've got lots of food. My grandpa is visiting from

Saskatchewan, and the whole family is coming over. You'll be fine." I push her in the direction of the back exit and she stumbles away, sniffing.

Outside, I unlock my bike. I wave at Franco, who ignores me as usual, then pedal casually around the building and find Topaz crouched behind a garbage can.

"I'd double you, but I don't have an extra helmet," I say. I get off my bike and pull on Topaz's arm. "Let's walk. He won't look for you at my house."

I try to sound ultra confident. I hope it is true.

Chapter Thirty-Three

Mom is in the kitchen rinsing baby spinach leaves. She takes one startled look at Topaz and says, "You brought home a friend, Pumpkin? That's nice, but you know today... "

She notices me shaking my head.

"Mom, this is Topaz. I think she needs to talk to you. She's being sexually harassed by Franco."

Mom wipes her hands on a towel, puts an arm around Topaz and guides her into the bathroom, the only room in the house with a lock, which I hear snap into place.

I go to my room and change my clothes. I put on my new I Heart I t-shirt and tuck it into my jeans, which is a huge challenge: not only is there a lot of extra fabric, but I also need to be careful not to rub off my patch. Over top I slip on my quilted riding vest. No one's going to see anything through that. Then I go back to the kitchen, wash my hands in the sink and find the recipe my mom was using for Mediterranean Baby Spinach Salad. It's an old family favourite, from before the time of metric measurement. All of the main ingredients are already on the counter. I chop up four hardboiled eggs and a red pepper, halve the cherry tomatoes, crumble the feta, drain a large can of garbanzos and find a jar to shake up the dressing. That's when I realize that Mom has doubled the recipe, so I have to double the ingredients for the dressing. Are four teaspoons the same as one tablespoon? Is a quarter cup the same as four tablespoons? I hate numbers anyway, but Imperial measurements are downright stupid. I'm surprised everyone didn't starve to death back then.

"Where is everybody?" asks Dad. He tucks a bottle of champagne into the back of the refrigerator, and tries to find space for a second bottle waiting on the kitchen table. "There's never any room in here," he says.

I'm holding the measuring cup up to the light struggling to see the marking lines against the olive oil. "Mom and Topaz are in the bathroom having a counselling session, and Grandpa and Isobel are decorating their condo."

What have I done? I pour the olive oil into the shaker jar; my grip is wobbly, so some of the oil drizzles down the side. Is that a teaspoonful? Is it too much to hope that Dad was distracted and not paying attention to what I said?

"What condo?" he says.

I've made a huge mistake. But I Heart I.

I face him. I will not cry. "It was supposed to be a secret. They bought a condo at the seniors village. That's what the big announcement is going to be."

Dad pulls out a chair and sits at the table. He stares at the champagne. "I bought four bottles of this stuff." He peels off the foil top, loosens the wire cage and twists the cork. Before he can drink it from the bottle, I pass him a coffee mug. "Why don't you get one for yourself too?" he says.

Foam spews out of the bottle as soon as Dad frees the cork. He pours us each half a mug full, and froth rises to the rim.

Champagne is pretty good, even at room temperature from a coffee mug.

"How did you find out?" says Dad.

"By accident. I was taking a shortcut through the seniors village and they were coming out of an Open House."

Dad nods. "They'll be living three blocks away."

I sip my champagne. Bubbles go up the back of my nose.

Dad says, "Well, at least they won't be needing our guest room any more. And visits will be brief, not days and days on end."

"I'm happy they'll be here. Grandpa's getting old."

Dad says, "I'm probably a grouch for saying this, but I don't enjoy weddings. They're a terrible waste of money. People are better off paying down their mortgages."

There—he's back to normal.

I have about three seconds to breathe, and then the doorbell rings. Dad makes no sign of reacting, so I answer it myself.

There on my doorstep is Logan Losino. Behind him, parked on the side of the road, is Franco's car.

"I'm sorry, Sylvia." Logan looks miserable. I've never seen him this sad or angry, or whatever he is. Maybe *sangry* would be a good word. "Franco made me bring him here. He's looking for Topaz. He thought she might have come home with you after your course. If she's not here, we'll leave."

"And if I tell you she's not here, you'll have to spend the rest of the day driving around with Franco in a bad temper looking for her?"

"That's about right," says Logan. "He's on a mission."

"And if she is here?"

"I'm supposed to give her the message that we're waiting for her, then go back to the car."

"He is such a bonehead," I say.

Logan shrugs. "I'm sorry. I couldn't make him stop screaming at me."

Now he looks helpless. I wish I could bring him into the house without further enraging Franco. Then I have a brilliant idea. "Logan, it's okay. I have a plan." I ignore his doubtful expression. "I'm going to hug you and haul you into the house. Can you try to make that look believable? Because obviously it isn't, I'm way too small to drag you anywhere."

Logan ponders the idea. "I could pretend you caught me off balance," he says.

"This will be fun," I say.

I fling myself at him. He staggers back against the railing as I pin myself to his chest. Both my feet are off the ground. My nose is pressed against his neck just below his ear. I hate to admit it, but he smells as wonderful as a horse. My insides feel all gooey again, even more than last time. It is the most luxurious sensation, I would like to do this forever. When can I make it happen again?

I feel his heart beating. He must feel mine.

"Should I put you down?" whispers Logan.

"I guess that was the plan," I say with reluctance.

There's a pause, then he drops me, I grab his arm, drag him into the house and slam the door. "That will buy us some time."

"I'm not complaining," says Logan.

Dad is still in the kitchen, bent over the salad recipe. Two juiced lemon halves lie flattened on the cutting board. He tightens the lid on the shaker jar and jiggles it back and forth.

"Dad, this is my friend Logan, and we need to get Mom out of the bathroom."

Dad shakes Logan's hand.

"Sorry about the olive oil," says Dad. He wipes his hands on a towel and passes it to Logan. Logan says it's no problem.

"Logan's brother Franco is outside in his car. He's stalking Topaz," I say.

Dad grows an inch or two in height. "I'll handle that," he says. "Not on my property." His chest expands.

"Wait a minute, Dad. Franco's not like Logan, he's not... "

"Skinny," says Logan.

I think about correcting him, but decide this is not the time. I hear the bathroom door snap open. "Dad, Franco's a jock. He's really big, and he's mean."

Dad hesitates. I think I've made my point but he says, "I'll take a baseball bat."

Mom says, "No one's playing baseball today." She ushers Topaz into the kitchen, which is feeling pretty crowded. Mom eyeballs me. "What on earth are you wearing, Pumpkin? You can't—"

I tell her that Franco is outside, waiting in his car.

Mom sighs. "I had hoped this could wait until Topaz's parents returned home, but apparently that won't be possible. I have a statutory duty to report when a child is at risk." She picks up the phone and dials 911.

Chapter Thirty-Four

Mom and a police officer are in the master bedroom with Topaz, who is giving her statement. Dad and another officer are in the kitchen discussing retirement financial strategies. Two more officers are outside interrogating Franco. Logan is in the family room talking to his parents on the phone.

The doorbell rings.

I peek out the living room window. Standing on the front steps are Mr. Brumby and Ms. Teke, the school counsellor. She is rubbing his arm soothingly.

Mr. Brumby is looking with concern at the two police cars. I guess I won't have to worry about him misbehaving. I wonder if I'll have any opportunity to take Ms. Teke aside and ask her what she thinks she's doing, hanging out with Mr. Brumby. Then again, she's an adult. She can take care of herself. I have enough on my hands.

I let them in and suggest they take a seat in the living room. I bring them the cold bottle of champagne from the refrigerator and two nice glasses. I find a bag of salt and vinegar potato chips in the pantry and give them that too.

I'm on my way to find napkins when Auntie Sally blasts in the front door with Taylor. Erika trails behind, plugged into her ear buds and iPod as ever. She is trying to look bored and disinterested, but her eyes dart around like little fishes in a bowl.

"This is exciting!" says Auntie Sally. "Are there policemen everywhere?"

"Dad's talking to one in the kitchen," I say.

Auntie Sally charges off, babbling about men in uniform.

"What's happening?" says Taylor. "What's Franco doing outside with the cops?"

"Topaz is here. Franco was stalking her. Mom called 911."

"Sadly, I always knew it would come to this," says Taylor.

"I'll be in your bedroom if anyone wants me," says Erika, walking away. She doesn't ask for permission, but it's easier to let her go.

The police finish with Topaz and take Franco away. Topaz agrees to stay in my mom's custody for the rest of the weekend until her parents are home. Mom says that being a helping professional expedited the process, otherwise Topaz could have been apprehended by Social Services and dropped in a foster home. I might have preferred that option to sharing my bedroom with Topaz; though on the other hand, I Heart I, so it's easier to be generous and understanding.

Dad fires up the barbecue and finds space in the refrigerator for two more bottles of champagne. I'm surprised and pleased that he still thinks there is anything to celebrate.

We ask Logan to stay for burgers, but he insists on going home to comfort his parents. Logan is a good person. I'm going to hang on to him. I take him to the front door to say goodbye.

Logan says, "If I ever have a kid like Franco, I'm going to put him up for adoption as soon as possible."

My heart sinks. I've been so selfish thinking about having puppies instead of babies. I'd given no thought to what a future husband might want.

"What's wrong?" says Logan.

If I tell him I can't have children will he drop me like a stone? He's fifteen—will family planning matter yet? Just because I know exactly what I want (horses, a dog maybe, more horses) doesn't mean Logan will have his own life as specifically mapped out. Then again, he might. Maybe he will dump me and take up with Topaz. She could be hugging him instead.

I cast my eyes down. I see the big red heart in the middle of my t-shirt. The two *I*'s are hidden behind my vest. Only I know.

"Sylvia? Did I say something wrong?"

"I probably can't have kids, because of the Turner Syndrome."

"Oh. Really? I didn't know that."

"Yeah, well... " I won't look at him.

He takes my hand. "Do you care, Sylvia? Do you want to have kids?"

His touch is very distracting, and I have difficulty coming up with a quick answer to his question. "I don't know. Sometimes I think I do. Other times I want puppies and kittens." I take a deep breath, gathering my courage, and search his face. "What about you?"

"Me?" says Logan. "I want to graduate from high school and become a professional mountain bike racer."

Obviously, he hasn't given fatherhood much thought. For now, my infertility isn't a reason for Logan to lose interest in me and take up with Topaz, or anyone else with fully functioning ovaries. Still, it could happen at any time. I'll always be vulnerable on this point, no matter what protective clothing I wear. People are weird about babies. Kansas and Declan expressed no interest in them at all, but then when Kansas got pregnant, having a baby became the most important thing in the world, even more important than horses.

"I can always adopt." I don't say *We*. I don't want to push him.

"Sure, as long as you're careful about not picking someone like Franco," says Logan.

I nod. I know he's making a joke to help me feel better, but I'm so emotional my throat feels like it's swelling shut.

"I can help you," says Logan. "I know all the early Franco-signs to look for."

I nod again. My heart leaps in my chest. He can help me. That's almost a *We*. And then because I can't talk and don't know what else to do, I untangle my hand from his and open the front door to let him out.

He steps past me, then stops, and I wonder what else he might have to say because his face is soppy and I know he doesn't really want to leave. Being at the front door must remind me of what happened earlier, because out of nowhere, I fling myself at him and he staggers back against the railing for real this time, so for an instant, I think we're going to topple over, but he steadies himself, and holds me and oh lord, I don't know what's happening to my body, but whatever it is, it must be good. Next week, I might put on two estrogen patches.

We would have stayed there forever if Grandpa and Isobel hadn't chosen that moment to pull into the driveway in their rental car.

I tell Logan to put me down. He skips away down the road.

I follow Grandpa and Isobel into the living room. My mom sees them and checks her watch. "It's seven o'clock," she says accusingly, though with everything else going on up until now, I'm sure she'd forgotten all about them.

Grandpa says, "Oh, we took a nap and overslept."

"Where on earth did you take a nap?" says Mom.

Grandpa takes Isobel's hand. "That's our surprise announcement. We bought a new condo," he says.

"You're not getting married?" says Mom.

Grandpa says, "We're already married, Ev. We went to a Justice of the Peace months ago. We didn't want a big fuss. And with real estate being more expensive on the coast than it is in Saskatchewan, we needed to be sure we had enough money. We don't want a mortgage at this stage in our lives."

Dad says, "We can't argue with that, can we Ev?" He drapes an arm around her and pulls her close. She crumples against him.

Mr. Brumby clambers out of the couch, where he has been nesting with Ms. Teke. I have been related to him for months without knowing, so I don't suppose anything needs to change now. He raises an empty glass and says, "I think this calls for more champagne." Which is about the nicest thing I've ever seen him do.

Isobel says, "Oh, Eddie, I'm so glad you're happy about all this."

I knew it. *Eddie.* I am totally creeped out.

Isobel flies across the room and hugs him. "And who's this lovely creature you've brought with you?" she asks, eyeing Ms. Teke.

Mr. Brumby introduces them. When he looks at Ms. Teke, he has that soppy expression I don't understand, but she doesn't seem to mind at all.

The phone rings. Mom grabs it, listens for a few seconds and passes it to me, then hovers.

"Hey, Sylvia," says Kansas. Her voice is weak. I'm immediately terrified.

"Kansas. How are you? How is the baby?" Taylor sidles up and squeezes my shoulder. I put my free hand on top of hers.

"We're fine. We had a false start, but now we're great. Really."

"But you sound sad," I say.

"I'm tired, that's all. And Sylvia... I'm sorry, there's one more thing."

What would she have to be sorry about? I'm relieved she's alive, and the baby is healthy. Then she tells me.

"It's a boy."

A boy. How crushingly devastatingly disappointing. "But the tests?"

"Apparently errors like this happen from time to time. He's perfectly normal. Sorry. No little sister for you." She waits a moment while I try to think of something appropriate to say. "Declan and I are very happy," she prompts.

"Congratulations. I'm happy for you."

"I knew you would be," says Kansas.

Chapter Thirty-Five

Topaz sleeps on a foamy beside my bed. She snores. At first I am annoyed. I roll over to watch her and think about reaching out with my foot and giving her a good nudge to wake her up, but this seems too much like kicking her, and that would not be right. I can clearly see her bald spot because she was frightened of the dark and Mom plugged in my old night light that I haven't needed since I was about two. She's wearing a t-shirt of my mom's (obviously mine would have been too small, except for I Heart I, and there's no way she's having that one). Her shoulder has popped out of the neck hole, and she's lying with her head on her hand. Even asleep, she looks sad. I listen to her breathing for a while, then I slide out of bed, tiptoe to the family room and turn on the computer. Facebook has a new message for me from Lygia Sanches. I don't know anyone with this name. I think about putting the message in the trash, in case it's from an Internet stalker. But curiosity gets the better of me and I open it.

Hi Sylvia. How are you? I saw your post on the TS Sistas site. My name is Lygia and I live in Brazil. I have Turner Syndrome too. I am older than you (22) but I remember what it was like to be 15. The main thing to know is that no one can tell you what you can and cannot do just because you have TS. You can do whatever you want. After I was diagnosed ten years ago, I decided I wanted to be a doctor. It took me three tries, but I am now in medical school. Follow your passion. You can write to me if you like. Welcome to the Sistas, Lygia.

Oh. My. God. I have met someone else with TS.

I have to open another screen before I find a way to reply. My fingers are trembling so much that it's difficult to type.

Hi Lygia. Thanks for writing. I am very excited, you are the first person I have ever met who has TS other than myself. Just wondering, did you have trouble with math? My passion is to join a horse circus, hopefully with my pony, Brooklyn, who is white and looks a lot like a Lusitano. I know a lot of Lusitanos are bred in Brazil—I suppose it's too much to expect that you have one yourself? I also have a boyfriend named Logan. Love, Sylvia.

I close the computer and make my way back to bed. Despite my excitement and Topaz's snoring, eventually I fall asleep and find myself dreaming. I am standing on two white horses, one bare foot on each bum. Their bridles and reins are as fine as spiders' webs. We are cantering in a huge circle. I draw back my right pinkie and the forehead of the right horse tilts into view.

"Don't ask me to turn the other way or I'll stab Brooklyn in the eye," says the unicorn.

I merge the two steeds into one.

Brooklyn tosses his head, and we canter over a small jump while I stand balanced on his back. I use my energy to speed him up and my breath to slow him down. My thighs are aching.

Spike trots up beside us with Taylor aboard. Taylor is laughing. "Spike wants to go for a long trail ride, then come home and have a big dinner. He wants some of Brooklyn's green hay. He says he's tired of that yellow straw Kansas gives him all the time." Taylor has attached a couple of lead ropes to Spike's halter and is using the ropes as reins. She's sitting on a bareback pad instead of a saddle. It's a start.

In the morning after breakfast, Grandpa and Isobel drive me and Topaz to the stable. We pick up Taylor on the way.

I'm not crazy about sharing my horse time with Topaz, but Mom gave me a *Don't-you-even-think-about-it* look when I started to object, so I am making an effort to be gracious.

Grandpa says they'll be back to pick us up in two hours. He and Isobel want to spend the morning at Home Depot looking at major appliances and area rugs. They act like it will be the most fun in the world to pick out a new stove. Beats me.

Topaz makes a bee-line for the barn, with Taylor hot on her heels, warning her not to try patting Hambone.

Kansas is standing in the doorway of her little house with a bundle in her arms, waving for me to join her.

She lifts the blanket from his head. "Sylvia, meet Aidan," she says.

Aidan looks like a monkey.

Kansas's facial expression is a galaxy beyond mushy.

"He's adorable," I lie.

"Oh, thank you, Sylvia. I know. He's perfect, isn't he?"

"Oh, yes," I say.

"Do you want to hold him?"

"Not today, thank you." I've been practicing with dolls at the babysitting course, but they're not the same as this vulnerable package of warm pinkness. I can't imagine holding him, let alone performing CPR.

"Okay," says Kansas. She doesn't mind. She'd rather hold him herself.

Bernadette is watching us from the living room, thumping her tail hopefully. She croons a small howl, and Kansas tells her to hush. I slip past and stroke her head.

"Kansas, where's your mom?" I ask over my shoulder.

"Declan's driving her to the bus depot. Her friend Miriam broke a hip, so she's gone to help out."

"I don't want to get old," I say.

"Miriam tripped on a toning stick in her Zumba class," says Kansas, as though that explains anything. "My mom will be back for a visit in a month or so—a short visit. She wants to stay in touch with her grandson."

"My grandpa is moving here," I say. "Not for a visit— permanently," I add, because I'm not sure Kansas is paying attention.

"That's nice," says Kansas. She traces Aidan's ear with her fingertip, then brings his head close to her nose and inhales deeply.

"I'm going to join a circus," I say out loud for the very first time.

"Mmmm," says Kansas.

"I'll see you later," I say. I give Bernadette one last pat, and head back to the barn.

Topaz is stroking Hambone's neck as the old grouch

leans out over his stall door. "I like this one," she says. He gently explores her hair with his muzzle. So much for being a notorious bully, or pretending to be. They are acting like long-lost kindred spirits. "If I had enough money, this is the horse I would buy," she whispers.

"Maybe you can work something out," I say. "He's Kansas's horse, but she won't be riding for a while. And you're going to be making money babysitting. Maybe you could lease him."

"Really?" says Topaz. Her eyeballs are ready to fall out of her head.

"You never know," I say.

Taylor calls me to the tack room where she's scanning the saddle racks. "Do you know which saddle would fit Spike? I don't need a bridle, I'd prefer bitless anyway, and he'll be good in his halter. I'd rather not use a saddle either, but I don't think I can balance bareback just yet."

Kansas's old bareback pad is tucked in the corner but I decide Taylor isn't ready for that yet either. "Take my saddle," I say. "I'll ride Brooklyn bareback today. There are a few things I want to try."

If I want to follow my passion, I need to start practicing.

Acknowledgements

When I began writing the *Born That Way* series, I knew nothing about Turner Syndrome. The first books were written largely with the help of academic research. I am grateful to the Turner Syndrome Society of Canada for inviting me to their annual conference where I was able to meet dozens of girls and women with TS, along with family members and researchers. I was deeply touched by the willingness of people to tell me their personal stories. It was an opportunity and an experience I will never forget.

Thanks to my publisher, Randal Macnair at Oolichan Books, for continuing to believe in Sylvia and me.

Thanks to my editor, Carolyn Nikodym, not only for her keen editing skills, but also for her sense of humour, thoughtfulness, and flexibility on the inevitable comma issues.

Thanks to Helen Austin for her song, "Always Be A Unicorn." I cannot imagine a more appropriate anthem for Sylvia, or better inspiration for me.

As always I am grateful to Mike who kept the home fires burning while I was lost in the garret.

Susan Ketchen pursued a wide range of careers, from financial policy analyst to family therapist, before focusing her attention on writing novels. Her fiction reflects her ongoing interest in relationships, health, family dynamics, animals and humour.

Her four-volume *Born That Way* series features a fourteen-year-old girl with two conditions: she has Turner Syndrome, and she is a horse nut. Although Susan does not have TS herself, she admits to the horse problem. Fortunately she was also born a writer, and by all accounts was observing and making mental notes from the very beginning. Writing has been and continues to be a joy, a trial, and at times a lifeline.

She lives in the Comox Valley on Vancouver Island, B.C., on a hobby farm with her husband, her good friend Lollipop (above left) and an assortment of cats and chickens.

Readers can find Susan online on Facebook or at www.susanketchen.com.

Lose yourself in Sylvia's world

Born That Way

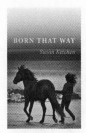

Sylvia is fourteen but stuck with the body of an eight-year-old. This might not be such a problem if Grandpa hadn't promised to buy her the horse she's always wanted, but only when she grows as tall as his shoulder.

Made That Way

Sylvia has begun medical treatment for her genetic disorder, but as usual not all goes according to plan. Sylvia must develop a deeper understanding of what "normal" means, and decide how important it is to get there.

Grows That Way

The dauntless Sylvia continues to explore the ebb and flow of herd dynamics, whether they arise in family life, schoolyard politics, or the paddocks of Kansas's stable.

More Praise for

Born That Way
    Made That Way
        Grows That Way

"Vancouver Island resident, lifelong equestrian and former family therapist Susan Ketchen draws on her considerable knowledge base and her passions for *Made That Way*. ...It's an engaging coming-of-age story that explores difference and personal growth through a variety of lenses. ...Ketchen has created a cast of quirky yet real characters who are easy to identify and empathize with. ...Ketchen demonstrates a clear understanding of the sometimes confused way young adults learn from and are impacted by the actions and interactions of those around them. ...Most YA readers will want to spend as much time as they can in Sylvia's world."
   - *The Globe and Mail*

"It makes such a big difference to read a book where they get the details right. The horses have personalities that are as real and quirky as the human characters and their interactions with their people are completely believable."
   - Nikki Tate, award-winning author and freelance broadcaster

"Wonderful. Reads like a cross between Adrian Mole and The Curious Incident of the Dog in the Night-time."
~ Dr. David Davies, Child and Adolescent Psychiatrist

"I love Susan's tone. There's lots of angst, but no self-pity, and lots of humour... the love and respect for horses is actually rather overwhelming. ...It's a rather unique YA text."
~ Kieran Kealy, Professor Children's Literature, UBC

"...engaging, wise and often very funny."
~ InFocus Magazine

"Quirky and relevant."
~Anna Blake, award-winning author and horse advocate

"...fast-paced, compelling and full of surprises. ..Sylvia's persistence and creativity in overcoming her life's challenges will inspire the reader for a lifetime."
~ Horses All

"The best books targeted at adolescents don't just offer escape from the pressures of changing bodies and a changing world; they offer an education on topics that young people are too shy or uncomfortable to broach. That is exactly what Born that Way does. Sylvia's growth—or lack thereof—combined with her mother's Freudian leanings leads her on a journey of self exploration that includes sexuality (an escapade with barnacles makes her wonder if she might somehow be a hermaphrodite), individuality, honesty, promise-keeping, and more."
~Northwest Horse Source